Bob Macaulay offers herein a forensic dozen, flap-wrapped, of stories & sketches, in which myth, medicine, romance, quasi-imperial dogs & mixed media pile on each other; precariously, to erect a true leaning Babel of affectionate piss-taking & parody, all the while leading sacred cows to the slaughter."

Bob began by qualifying in medicine at Edinburgh University and then worked as a lecturer there. His grandfather was also a medical student, in the same year as Conan Doyle, and like his fellow student, told many a tale about the extraordinary deductive observational skills of Professor Joseph Bell on whom Conan Doyle based Sherlock Holmes. Bob did his pathology residency at Stanford University medical school in California, then wrote journal articles and chapters in standard text books. A passion for theatre brought him back to the Edinburgh Fringe Festival. After a premature academic burial at the University, offered to him as early retirement, he got an actors' union Equity card while writing and acting with the Edinburgh Playwrights Workshop, which performed, several of his plays. He's a keen cyclist and plays in a street busking group called Ukes Against Nukes, whose music is described as "the broken lorry sound" but it gets its message to us quite well.

SATIRIC SLICES FROM SCOTLAND
THE DOCTOR IS IN!
AND HIS EVERY BLADE A BLEEDER.

the series

Shaggy Coo Hoots·tm

Incisions
2019

Scissor & Bone
2020

The Hapless Tweaser
2021

SinisterGrams
2022

C-Sections
2023

"Inviting the spider out
for a laugh and a stout"

San Francisco, Santa Fe, Edinburgh, Paris

Incisions

BOB MACAULAY

firefall[tm]

For their encouragement, I thank my family and friends, especially the Scottish writers Mary Gladstone and George Gunn, during the decades in which this "work" accumulated and to my editor for his inspired tactful impertinence.

First Edition: February 2019
hardcover: 978-1-939434-62-3
paper-bound: 978-1-939434-63-0

design & editorial:
Elihu Blotnick

cover: Heilan' Coo
(Scotland: variant for haiku)

firefall originals-ᵗᵐ

literary@att.net
www.firefallmedia.com

SURGICAL SATIRES
(TO WIT)

Up the Spout

The famous foursome are taken aback when confronted with a puzzling and discomforting situation while on holiday with their Uncle Jack in Bog O'Bigbog, a remote rain-swept region of the Scottish Highlands. Starting with a dog's dinner under canvas, their adventures lead them in the dead of night into the Forest of Fucksakesnoe to the Spout of Glen Snottie on a raised beach above Prawn Bay. Where they uncover a vile plot to rot the very Fabric of Society. After many thrills and spills the danger is eventually overcome, in appalling weather, by means of Uncle Jack's surface-to-air guided Cigars and an inflatable Liver Transplantation unit. A hair-raising Tale.

fIVE UNDER THE WEATHER

NOW THAT BOBBY had reached the age of ten, he hoped he might get taken on as a fifth member of the famous four. But the Fab Five was not yet to be; not for now at any rate.

To start with, his twin cousins had always secretly despised him for being such a weed and thereby getting bigger helpings of bread and butter pudding on their summer holidays together. And Napoleon the dog had remained aloof and indifferent since Bobby's hobbled arrival off the ferry that morning.

Only Georgina stood up for him, reminding her younger brothers, as she brushed back her tousled hair, that cousin Bobby's limp was due to an in-bred club foot, running down his mother's side of the family from a distant forbear. Rumored to have been an orphan and left out to dry at low tide, but miraculously rescued by a band of furtive playwrights smuggling in fountain pens and the latest scrunchy knitwear. To the twins' mind, this tale lent an odour of almost diabolic notoriety to Bobby's disability that it might not otherwise have had.

Outside their terraced family bothy on the Bog O' Bigbog, the wet earth was drying in the summer wind and all the sea was green. Just then Uncle Jack burst in via the back entrance, a giant peapod of a man and the local GP, fresh from an all-night Fiscal post-mortem.

Napoleon, ears up, slid off his master's chair at the breakfast table where the family were clustered and made for the remains of a stiff rabbit in his basket. Sniffing his master's trousers as he passed, he gave them a wide berth because they smelled of a decomposed body left out for a week up on the bald wind-swept Scrags of Dunbumman.

"Right," growled Uncle Jack, fixing himself a stiff gin-and-tonic, throwing himself into a chair and lighting a black Balkan Sobranie cigarette. "I'd better down cook's porridge and get some double shut-eye. What mischief are the five of you going to get up to to-day?"

Napoleon would've wagged his tail had he not been sitting on it.

Fanny the cook wiped her hands on a tear stained apron and hovered uncertainly with a poached egg plate. "They're taking Napoleon and a picnic lunch down to Loch Mess then over the old drover's road to Rubha Roddie."

"Yes," blurted one the twins, "then we'll make for the bus stop at Lochan Gotcha, that is if Bobby can keep step with us"

"Otherwise we've planned to pitch boot camp in the woods at Tossie Mick" blurted the other.

"I'll do it, you'll see" blurted Bobby too. "I'm now a full scout and I've started doing press ups and upper body grills. My new teacher Miss Givings says..." He would've gone on but the twins were getting down from the table and Uncle Jack had noddled off in his spottled cravatte.

Nonetheless, the scraping of chairs on the tiled kitchen floor woke Uncle Jack with a start and he stormed through to his bedroom, drawing the black curtains and making sketches of them too. He wasn't as young as he once was and probably would have a liver transplant to do later on that day, if a suitable donor could be found.

"Take these with you," said cook, brightly putting two maps in Georgina's ruc-sac alongside the cheese and potted meat sausages. She waved them off as they left, whimsically wiping a tear from her one remaining eye as she did so.

No sooner had the five set briskly off down the upper road than the rain came pissing down. But in their hearts, lapwings larked in the bottled sky, Peedie blossom scented the breeze and the sea was as evergreen as ever.

After a good soaking, they cut their journey a bit short and pitched their new tent poles beneath the spreading oaks of the Forest of Fucksakesnoe.

The five get Tucked up with Tunnocks

"FIRST NIGHT in a tent on your own, eh?" beamed Georgina approvingly. She liked reading Bobby to sleep in his younger days when they shared a tent. "Maybe you'd like Napoleon to keep you company. He can't stay out all night in this weather."

"But he's as soaked as the rest of us." said Bobby.

"If we give you the biggest tent then Napoleon can curl up in the space between the inner and the outer and you'll keep each other warm. I know what," Georgina continued in her knowing sort of a way, "Let's say that whoever has Napoleon in the tent with them gets an extra sausage."

"That's two extras, if it's us," said the twins quickly.

"You'd each have half a single," Georgina insisted, her eyes flashing and high cheek bones aglow.

"No way. Let kid Bobby have it," they twinned, "He can put Napoleon to sleep reading him the Boy Scout's manual by match light."

"I've brought two packets of caramel wafers," Bobby replied evenly. "Mum said to be sure and share them out."

"After the sausages or while they're cooking?" enquired Georgina with one eyebrow.

"She didn't say."

"If we have'm before supper, we'd have to let the dog eat some as well," one of the twins pointed out, his eyes narrowed.

"And as he's probably never had a Tunnocks Caramel Wafer in his life before. Better leave the dog out of it," the taller twin pointedly asserted.

Georgina said an occasional wafer probably wouldn't do Napoleon any harm as he often mangled raw rabbits after all.

And as often happened to the five after a stiff day's hike in the open, hunger came on in unrelenting waves like breaking surf. Both packets of wafers were gone before the sausages were half ready.

Outside, the moon was split and obscured by bantering

hummocks of grey green cloud. Inside, potted meat sausages with cheese and caramel wafers washed down with cans of Locozade caused a drowsy numbness to pain the senses of the five and swiftly sweep them into the land of nod. Except for Napoleon that is, who in most things that mattered of course was essentially non-human.

Napoleon was having a disturbed night due to the intake of several unaccustomed caramel wafers before his proper dinner and was thus easily woken by a clap of thunder. In the silence following, he heard, with the naturally enhanced hearing of his species, a distinct whistling, short lasting, then several more.

Fully aroused, and needing a poo anyhow due to a caramel over-dose, he squeezed under the slackened outer tent between pegs, pood and sniffed the air. The rain stopped. There was that whistling sound again, softer, longer; with the curiosity and iron will of his Corsican counterpart, he made off towards its source.

As the forest got thicker and darker, Napoleon was able to thread his way through it at some speed because his night vision was unnaturally enhanced by under-the-cover slurps of Bobby's sugary Locozade. Eventually the forest abutted onto a flat raised beach by the Spout of Glen Snottie, overlooking Prawn Bay, where a cylindrical tent made of militarily camouflaged material was being inflated by an air pump. This had a leak in it which emitted under high pressure an occasional whistling sound inaudible to the machines's merely bi-pedal operators, but not to a super-sonically alert French poodle with a bit of hound dog up against the wrong side of the family tree.

And there was a submarine anchored a little way out in the bay from which inflated rafts with men clad from top to toe in black serge were bringing ashore all kinds of gear on wooden pallets and humping them up and into the tent.

With the utmost stealth, Napoleon crept nearer but kept his distance till all the men were inside, whereupon he moved in closer and hid himself behind one of the pallets leaned up against the outside of the tent. Above him, he saw a gap in the tent wall where two flaps had failed to overlap properly, and in a flash he was up on the pallet, flat out along its top edge and looking down through the gap onto full blown operating theatre geared up and ready for a liver transplantation.

Napoleon's Night Out at the Theatre

Two trolleys were wheeled in from either end of the tent, each carrying an inert human body lying on its back with sheets identically arranged to expose only the upper abdomen. One body, slightly pinker than the other, had someone attending to a rubber mask at its head end. The other body was unattended and looked a good deal less pink.

Then four more folks came on the scene, these done up in green dressing gowns and wearing caps and face masks that made them look like bank robbers Napoleon had seen on a DVD back home in Bog O'Bigbog. And in no time the greens were plunging scalpels into the prone abdomens, two to each one, each pair looking as if they were doing exactly the same thing. The air released from the vent smelled a bit peculiar to Napoleon but the lighting was first class. Good enough for him to see long curved incisions being made from of the lower end of the breast bone down to the right, parallel with the rib cage, and Stunner's clips placed over the common hepatic artery and portal vein which were in turn severed and both ends secured with nylon brassed bands. The three larger and two smaller hepatic veins were then located and similarly ligated. After which the common bile duct was divided and both ends tied off with sutures of fine catgut. That was nearly more than Napoleon could endure, but he persevered too.

After the diaphragmatic ligament had been secured with horned forceps, Napoleon, salivating a bit, watched as both livers were removed from their bodies at the same time by one pair of rubber gloves while the other pair retracted the rib cage with a moistened "Joe's Hoe" to enlarge the operative field.

The smaller nobbly liver from the better coloured abdomen got chucked in a stainless steel bucket and the larger, smoother purpler liver from the paler body was promptly sown into the pinker one, by the exact same procedure used for its removal in reverse.

After a bit of stitching up, and the two trolleys wheeled back down the canvas tunnel in the respective directions from which they came, Napoleon made out the paler body, now looking more marbly white, being pushed into what looked like a home fridge door but was big enough to accommodate the trolley and on-lying body being trundled into it.

As for the double fastenings of the door, the throwing of switches, the red lights flashing on and off and the low hum of a mobile electric cremator starting up, Napoleon saw and heard it all; but knew he was going to have trouble conveying these impressions to his four sleeping companions with the limited repertoire of woofs at his disposal.

Yet, he was going to try. They'd be SO intrigued. He soon made his way back through the forest to the five's campsite by re-tracing the trail of own caramelised poos that he'd luckily dropped off, on the way out.

Back at the camp, woofs worked through, Napoleon added tearing the ground with his front feet in bone-burying mode, scampering about wildly and finally, a sure-fire wake-up call for Georgina's ears, intermittent whining. He wouldn't come into anyone's tent for comfort and was too active and vigorous to be in pain so she put on her clothes and got out of her tent to see what was what.

Napoleon straightaway vanished out of site into the forest and immediately came back again. pawed the ground, woofed twice and went off, in the same direction as before, and came back again just as soon. Now Bobby got up and out as well, just narrowly avoiding putting a bare foot into Napoleon's first Tunnock's caramel playback.

"It'll be a rabbit," the twins shouted up, not leaving their sleeping bags. "He's caught something and wants us to see."

"He'd be more likely to bring it to the camp," said Georgina, "that's what he usually does"

"He's done a giant poo right outside my tent," said Bobby. "Perhaps he's about to do another but can't make up his mind if and where."

This put the twins into gear and out of their bags, speaking as one: "Maybe he's pood an intact Tunnocks somewhere. ...Somewhere in the woods...That never touched his insides ...And wonders if we'd like him to retrieve it...Being largely undigested...For breakfast...Very good, Napoleon...It's all your fault, Bobby!"

"I'm going with him," said Georgina.

"Can I come too?" asked Bobby.

"We'll all go," said the twins.

"No," said Georgina sternly, "you two stay put and start the breakfast sausages."

"There aren't any...We scoffed the lot."

"Well in that case, all right then. But keep your eyes peeled for little Red Riding Hood."

Dawn inching over the Hough of Yell saw the five happily inventing other intestinal scenarios to which Napoleon might be leading them so sure-footedly.

But when they got to the raised beach by the Spout of Glen Snottie there was nothing there. Nothing to be seen at all. The entire canvas tunnel with everything in it had been taken back to the submarine. All that remained were fresh signs in the sand of heavy goods dragged ashore, up onto the raised beach and then back down again.

Napoleon was disappointed: there was nothing intriguing left to show off. He sniffled around, thinking he'd picked up traces of the unusual aroma he'd experienced when the surgery started. Suddenly the unexpected smell of a discarded cigarette end distracted him. He barked twice; loud ones, short and peremptory. Georgina went to him at once. Napoleon heard a sharp intake of breath when she saw that the fag-end he had stumbled upon was the remains of one of her Uncle Jack's Balkan Sobranies,

What on earth could Uncle Jack have been doing out here in this remote spot in the middle of the night, she wondered, and what could have caused the ground around the beach to be so scuffed and broken up?

Bobby probed around in a rock pool. The twins spun flatties into the sea. Georgina picked up the cigarette end, put it in her purse and the five returned to their camp, with Bobby saying that their whole trip up the Spout had been something of a wild goose chase, which managed, for once, to raise a grudging laugh from the twins. At last Bobby was showing signs of being ...well...not so...odd.

UNCLE JACK ON THE BUTTON

Back at the bothy that night in Bog O'Bigbog, the five gathered round the fire with Uncle Jack and their broiled Horlicks.

"Could this possibly be one of yours Uncle Jack?" tentatively asked Georgina, showing him the cigarette end.

"Yes, dear," he replied, "I think it is. So sorry. I do tend to leave them lying around. Just pop it in the fire".

Georgina took a deep breath. "Napoleon found it on the raised beach up by the Spout of Glen Snottie. We were camping by chance nearby in the forest of Fucksakesnoe. Absolute downpour all day. We cut our hike short."

Uncle Jack's took a deep breath too. "Can't be one of mine then. Was anyone with Napoleon at the time?"

"We were all there," said a twin.

"Really?...and...and...what else was there...was there anything else there...to see?"

Napoleon detected a slight tremor in his master's left hand on the arm of the sofa.

"No nothing at all," replied Georgina. "But the ground all around was a bit torn up. We wondered if you might've been involved in some kind of kerfuffle."

"Not me. No." averred Uncle Jack. "Lots of people smoke my brand. Could have been a picnic. People coming ashore and so on, presumably in better weather than at present. Ha ha. Thank you for your concern. Please. Just chuck it in the fire. Er...did any of you find...anything else...of interest...lying around...on the beach?"

"Yes," said Bobby, "I found this button in a rock pool. Shiny black. Couldn't miss it. A big one, like you might get off an overcoat. Here look, it's got a pattern of five little crowns pressed into it in a circle."

Napoleon saw his master's tremor swerve off-piste into a white knuckle of rigidity. With his free hand Uncle Jack reached out towards the button Bobby was holding, but he knew instinctively he shouldn't leave his fingerprints on it.

This button can only have come from the coat of that Rear Admiral whose liver we turned last night, he thought breathlessly. What a hopeless job the clean up squad must have done to leave stuff like this lying around. Heaven knows what other bits and pieces might still be out there.

Dark frowns etched his rugged features. If the Enemy were to find them, they'd be able to trace who we are...and worse... where we are. He'd have to alert the Authorities right away.

Action always put Uncle Jack's tremor on the back burner and, releasing himself from the arm of the sofa, he turned to Bobby and said with a spurious smile and without a trace of punctuation, "Look Bobby I've got a friend like you a little older who likes to wander about beaches picking up stuff that catches her eye which she brings home and sows them into quaint little baby's dresses and she'd love this button here tell you what I'll give you a tenner for it how's that?"

"Thank you Sir. She can have it. Your friend sounds fun."

"Very noble of you Bobby but please don't call me Sir, I'm

your Uncle Jack. Now you must excuse me for a moment children there's a call I've got to make to the hospital on the car phone and when I'm back I'm going to need your help. Trouble brewing up here it looks like I'm afraid get the Horlicks on again and I'll be back in a jiff and explain everything."

Outside in his bullet proof Bentley, Uncle Jack lifted the hot-line emergency phone embedded in the steering wheel centre: "10 Downing Street, Hullo. Prime Minister Yes. Looks like our latest...field...of operations...is in grave danger of being rumbled...pure chance...stray dog...picked up some bits and pieces left over from last night...damn poor show, for godsakes get the whole place cleaned up properly PDQ. There could be bits of the Rear Admiral's rotting liver lying about in the heather for all we know and heaven knows what else besides. How is he? Woken up you say. Good. Whose next? The Minister of Bereavement and Pest control? This is desperate, Prime Minister. The Enemy will stoop at nothing to clean out our last defences. To be on the safe side, we'll go on full alert up here at our end just in case. Well, cheers! Bend the knee for me when you're next with Brenda."

Uncle Jack sprang back into the bothy. "Right boys and girls, let's have a sit down, and Napoleon too. I'm going to have to tell you rather a long story. "Let's put more peats on the fire. Cook, you don't have to stay up."

A Queer Tale

Uncle Jack racked his brains to find a way of explaining the intricacies of the villainous trans-national plot that he and Her Majesty's Government was faced with; whose sole intent and purpose was to undermine the Very Fabric of Society. How to make this credible to primary school children; one of them hovering albeit on the hinge of puberty?

Many more peats were needed for Uncle Jack's tale.

18

Bobby found it the best story he'd ever met, better even than his well thumbed edition of "Bambi Returns to Blood Island." Napoleon was asleep in the lap of his new chum whose curiosity and Locozade he was beginning to appreciate.

The twins were totally taken up as well. They'd always felt between them they had the mind and body equivalent to at least one Tarzan. But their Uncle's unfolding exploits clearly needed a degree of grit, pluck and determination well beyond that required of the average strongman in a tropical rain forest.

Georgina, who was already bent on becoming a Red Cross Supervisor, easily picked up the bits about a deadly disease that had wiped out nearly half of Her Majesty's inner ruling elite. And that the only cure was emergency liver transplantation which is where uncle Jack came in, being a doctor and all.

But her thick curly hair got markedly touseled when it came to understanding why tainted cocoa at a United Nations Peace-keeping Conference had poisoned the British Delegation but no-one else, especially with the Russians manufacturing World Peace in their secret laboratories and openly sharing it.

For his part, Uncle Jack decided to leave out any reference as to why military clean-up operations were now increasingly outsourced to American seals due to austerity measures. With the official result that "the failure of which was one of the main causes impinging on setting the whole ball rolling". This would be hard enough to get past the befuddled House of Lords, let alone his four famously intelligent young relatives.

As for his written report to the Pharmaceutical Sponsors of his Transplant Research, Uncle Jack glossed right over having to procure fresh donor livers from persons recently in receipt of death penalties for Crimes Against Humanity and subsequently disposed of without trace.

In any case, transplant surgery was a cake-walk compared with finding a bottle of Jane Walker in a Glasgow off-licence.

Cook came in with some hot chocolate and a homely platter of "fly cemetery" Garibaldi biscuits, the raisins inserted by her very self that very afternoon. "Are you all staying up late or what?" she asked wearily, her eye-patch encrusted with flour.

"Looks like it, cook, but you don't have to. I've things to attend to and fortunately the children are all now old enough to be able to lend a hand. We'll take a short walk to refresh ourselves and then come back and get to work. You get to bed, cookie."

"So I will. Goodnight everyone."

DOWN IN THE BUNKER

With cook tucked into her sweet little converted sheep pen at the far end the bothy, Uncle Jack went to one of the old plates on display on the top-most shelf of the kitchen dresser and turned it slowly anti-clockwise with both hands. With a sinister creak, the lid of a trap door in front of the fire slowly opened up, lifting the quilted hearth rug with it.

Uncle Jack put a gnarled finger to his lips: total silence was now called for, as he ushered the five down stone steps that led to a sizable underground bunker excavated from the living rock. He followed them down the steps, closing the heavy trap door above him and flicking on the bunker's lights.

"Right, he said crisply, "this is the control room in the event of a surprise attack. It connects with other top secret underground bunkers concerned with…er…Nuclear Defence issues… Alien invasives…and over-consumerisation…things like that… including my on-shore liver research lab. We've got to hurry."

On a wall were TV screens over desks set up with dials and manual-control joy sticks with which the five were increasingly familiar now. The screens displayed views from hidden cameras pointed in all directions on the thatched roof of the bothy.

"You twins man those consoles," Uncle Jack added, "triggers on the left are for mounted machine guns. On the right, surface-to-air Cigars, our very latest guided missile. Georgina, you don these earphones and woman the tele-communications desk. Now your job, Bobby, will be to look after Napoleon, I don't want him barking and tearing about if all hell breaks loose, the balloon goes up, and the worst happens."

Uncle Jack's orders were interrupted by Napoleon doing exactly that. Barking, growling and dashing back up the steps towards the closed trap door. Very soon the smell that had so upset Napoleon became obvious to the others as well...the acrid fumes of chemical smoke.

"Ye God's," exclaimed Uncle Jack gritting his stained teeth with mounting vehemence, "the Enemy's broken into this complex at the other end and set my lab on fire, with all the hair-less rats in their cages. We've got to escape but the smoke's blocking the only way out and we can't pop up by surprise through the trap door in case cook's still up and about. She's already got one hernia as it is. Not that I gave it to her."

"What's that up there," Bobby said, pointing to a gap in the reinforced concrete ceiling of the bunker.

"It's for ventilation," croaked Uncle Jack, loosening his spot-tled cravat, "Its a natural fissure in the rock that connects up with the bottom of the peat stack outside."

It was very narrow, too narrow for the sturdy twins, and out of the question for Georgina. After a short silence, Bobby said he was probably still just small enough to squeeze up it if the twins got him up onto Uncle Jack's shoulders for an avuncular lift.

His new teacher Miss Givings had told him that upper body strength might come in just as handy as running and Bobby was up that fissure in the rock like a snake, edging aside peats from the bottom of the stack above him to get himself out.

He then hobbled to the back door of the bothy, burst in to the kitchen, banged a chair on the table, pushed the table against the dresser, clambered clumsily on top of the chair, and tip-toeing up on his good leg, reached the dresser's top plate with both hands and just managed to turn it like his Uncle had

21

done so a short while ago.

At that very moment two drones zoomed low over the Bog O' Bigbog, heading straight for the bothy, loaded with high and mighty explosives. Bobby was so relieved to see them both downed by his trusty cousins and Uncle Jack's Cigars, that he took no notice whatsoever of the prevailing weather conditions. Not that they'd changed noticeably much during the evening's excitement.

Uncle Jack and the others raced excitedly up the steps and hugged each other with relief.

"Phew that was a close shave...things were getting pretty hot...what a scrape...Bobby you were super...."

"You were all super," barked Uncle Jack, lighting a Balkan Sobranie and pouring himself a stiff gin and tonic. Napoleon licked his lips in agreement and in anticipation of any left over licks of tonic which there usually were.

They all had to agree, it was possibly a Tunnock's Caramel Wafer that began the process and saved the day in the end.

Months later, those members of the evil regime, within and without, at sea and on land, on the moors and in the forest, responsible for the attack were all rounded up and, after freely admitting their Crimes Against UK Humans, were shown judicial clemency. Instead of summary execution, they were given custodial sentences which included having to donate, at regular intervals, hefty parts of their livers to Uncle Jack's research lab, now off-shore and underwater, for the rest of their so-called natural lives.

Georgina, having been initiated into the Red Cross at a weekend's morbid anatomy and mythology intensive, was able to explain to the other children in awesome detail, far better than Napoleon, that the intervals between these gangsters' surgical ablations were to allow for what remained of their livers to recover and reach full size again before the next punishing extraction.

A Hapless Quest

A Feeling for Maths with Debbie

SOMEONE IN THE BIBLE, or could it be Einstein's mother, is said to have said that even thinking about coveting your neighbour's ass (which I take to mean fancying a shag in a divine kind of way) is, as far as hopes for redemption at the final whistle are concerned, tantamount to actually having enjoyed doing it, the whole hog, as it were, all the way, without a Permit.

But what if the coveted ass, in her full person, doesn't share this view; what if she doesn't mind being coveted one little bit, as long as it's from a long way off, of course. The problem never gets a mention in the Old Testament, it appears, or even in the new one. I don't think Einstein's mother would've remarked on my concern either if I'd not brought up the subject one evening round at her place over the chicken soup.

The thing is that, during maths lessons, staring out of the top floor window at Debbie's bum passing down the street on its way to Boots the chemist where she works, the unexpected always happens. Debbie can't possibly see me from here, or even know I exist, but it's as if she can actually feel something impacting on her behind the moment I start staring, as if my gaze is making real contact somehow, as if a bit of me, like a flea, is landing on her. And to prove it, often she reaches down and flicks it off, my unwelcome gaze, the very moment it alights.

What can she be feeling? How can she know what's in my mind? And how does this translate, three floors down and over a road, into something she senses like a misty rain?

All this was well beyond me until, as I say, covetousness, and, "it's as if you're already doing it", came up one evening round at the Einstein's, along with the large probability of it ruining any chance of a worthwhile resurrection.

But if so why, after the brush off, does she pull down the hem of her T-shirt by only one centimetre? Is this half measure expected to cool my fever and reduce her desirability? Will this square my circle? Teacher says I have a real feeling for maths.

Einstein's mother was about to speak to this point but did not; neither being a believer in quantum entanglement nor a denier of gravity.

Shall I Compare Thee to a Summer's Debbie?

I DECIDED to meet Debbie at the start of next term. Still at Boots the chemist she was, selling a packet of ribbed Durex to an older boy and laughing her head off, when I went in. Unreasonably tall she was too, as seen from the ground; her wide eyes and her black hair stood out above the slight white uniform she had on. Or was it my hair standing on end, in spite of the Brylcream dab? Yes, I should ask for something serious, for my feet.

"Sir?"

"I'll have some."

"What?"

"Of that...cream, please."

"For what, sir?"

"My head...er...I mean, feet."

"We don't do one for both, sir, in the same tube."

"I mean for the feet. I've got athlete's...foot."

"Yes, sir. Have you a prescription?"

"Yes, it's an itchy rash between the toes."

"Not a description, sir, a pre-scription, on a piece of paper. The doctor gives it to you."

> Do I have to write it down then, what
> it feels like to be so in love with you?

"I'll do it, yes, I will."

"No sir, you get it from your doctor."

> I'm not in love with the doctor.
> All I get from him is jabs.

"Well perhaps you could try this to start with. I sometimes use it after ice skating."

Her eyelashes curl like iron railings round a war memorial. Her lips are enormous. They billow out towards me like wave on wave of crimson surf.

Debbie on Ice: How Did Mum find Out?

"Ice skates?" asked Dad, "I thought you said you wanted a trombone for Christmas."

"I've been thinking of skating."

"But you can't skate at school. It's a ridiculous sport. No conceivable use whatsoever. Unless you're Norwegian."

"I'll save for the trombone myself then."

"Go on," Mum said warmly to Dad, "let him have a pair. They're a nice lot down at the ice rink. Dora gets the bus home with them after the hairdressers."

> *Was that a wink? Is Mum conspiring*
> *with me in secret?...does she Know?*
> *How the hell can she Know?*
> *How could she have Found Out?*

"He's keeping his hair tidier this year too. The headmaster thinks it's rubbing off on his written work also. Go on now."

"You know, Bunty, I think you're right. Especially as he'll be rather worn out and a lot less noisy about the house."

The fur Queue Tolls the Knell of Parting Debbie

I just don't understand, why doesn't everyone take up ice skating or tennis. I mean, those short skirts are sensational. A knock out. Good God! There Debbie goes skating backwards. Now what's the point of that? As Dad says, no conceivable use whatsoever, apart from the having to stick your bum out more in order to balance.

Ah, got it! Going backwards, she can check on the guys as they catch up with her, smoothing their hair with one hand and lightly touching her elbow with the other.

Now, she skids to a halt in mid-rink and just stands there, looking round, waiting for a suitable gap to develop in between the other skaters so she can let fly again with those fabulous legs. But at other times she just seems to be waiting...open...to offers....?

Right. Get feet parallel. Correct knock knees. Wait for one of her still moments. Then Push Off (firmly) from the wooden barrier round the edge of the rink...and as I get near her, Slow (fractionally), Grin (massively), Point (to the feet), giving her the thumbs up...then Stop (cooly but decisively), and ask her to Spend the Rest of her Life with me.

Not having practiced the Stop as much as the Push Off, I sail on, straight past her, waving both arms like a traffic policeman on a highway smeared with bacon fat.

Months on, I saw her at the January sales with a spectacular tan; queuing for a fur coat on the arm of an all-in wrestler, whose one arm is noticeably larger than any one my legs, both of them in fact.

I began to lose my feeling for maths.

WHICH ONE'S DEBBIE?
(Just how many are there?)

AT THE TENNIS CLUB. Everyone's newly grown up now and has left home. But we've all got short trousers on again. That's good.

But where's Debbie?

I'm feeling rather fit. Judy says so at the bike shop, just as it is closing. "I think you two'll get on."

Though it's just after Christmas, I get a tan at the sauna.

"Her ex-boyfriend is the cousin of my nephew Raymond. You remember, the one who had a terrible crush on Clarissa over there by the green door."

"OK yes. Got it. Raymond's...nephew's...cousin's...ex...that it? But which is Debbie?"

"That's her!"

"Who?"

"In the corner."

"There's two of them."

"The tall dark one."

"Talking to a short man in long shorts?"

"That's her."

"And shaking with laughter? She's so right, his shorts are hysterical."

We go over. "Debbie, this is Hamish: Hamish, Debbie."

"Hullo. Um. Nice here, isn't it? Look, can I hold your rackets for you, take the weight of them off your hands?"

"No thanks I'm just about to play."

"Yes, of course, no. As a matter of fact, so was I...."

> *Well, I was, but where the hell's the court?*
> *Where's Judy got to?*
> *So that was Debbie!*

Alternative Debbie

IMAGINE MY FEELINGS, getting a bit of a stiff neck in early middle age, when, at the bio-field chakra massage class last Saturday, suddenly there's Debbie, in trousers of curtain material, with a cashmere sweater, and a pink hair band. Will I get paired off with her. Can this be my lucky dyad?

No, it isn't. I'm allocated a stuffed school janitor, built like a millenium. Stiff, solid, rigid all over, from his iron nostrils to the toe-nails. I get a belly-ache relaxing his wrists. At lunch, his picnic explodes across the table for miles around. Eggshell, egg-jam, egg-butter and breadcrumbs everywhere, till he falls flat asleep. This means I get to have the instructress work on my neck, which is good. But standing up and sitting down in a chair over and again while she holds onto the back of my head is not, frankly, the sort of Alternative Therapy I had in mind when I signed on for this weekend. Especially as Debbie's now getting what's called cranio-sacral therapy on the floor right in front of me which looks and sounds like some kind of phantasy mid-wifery.

"Can I have what they're doing," I ask the instructress, "but for my shoulders? One of my collar bones has locked up and the other's turning blue."

"Try and release more," she replies.

> *More what? Legs already at full stretch and*
> *eyes sticking out like fighting dog's bollocks,*
> *concentrating at not looking at Debbie,*
> *as she's writhing about in front of me on*
> *the floor with her eyes wider than ever.*

> *Think I'll stay with milk-less milk that tastes of*
> *cardboard. And frequent changes of mouth wash.*

Debbie and the Big Question

FINALLY SITTING down with Debbie, at last. Unfortunately she's now half my age. It's been a long wait and we've only got seven minutes before the next customer's up the steps of her mock gypsy caravan parked in Princes Street gardens, near a mock High Street of mock Alpine Chalets only selling mock kebabs specially mocked up for MockMas.

She's Cosmic Debbie, astrologer, palmist and seer. Tall, dark, with a beaming smile and an invitation to cross her palm with silver. I'd cross it with a meal out and a seat for Handel's Messiah or any else's for that matter, she's so gorgeous. Should I give it a try? Perhaps, after the first seven minutes, if they go well, I can get another seven, this time with the....

"What d'ye call 'em?"

"Tarot Cards," Debbie murmurs, through a ton and a half of eye-liner.

And then ask to walk you back
to your place after closing time?

"What is your question?"

That's a good one. How do some people
always seem to be able to read my mind?

"For the Cards?"

"Oh yes, of course, yes. Mmmm."

"Okay, will I be a lonely old git, or will I have an intimate relationship with a wide-eyed raven-haired beauty, a fabulously dishy woman whose high cheek bones, sense of purpose and skill at cards delights me and devotes me to her. And who incidentally laughs heartily at my jokes?"

"That's a bit of a tall order," she says with a smile. "But least we have your birth data."

"Let's start with the bit about the lonely git and leave the dishes till later."

Debbie Progessional Relations in Tunnochbrae
(Nurse Debbie's initiative. Safety Faust)

"We've an outbreak of syphilis in Tunnochbrae, nurse Debbie."

"Oh! Doctor McMoodie, whatever next?"

"Nurse, er...will you, er would you...come here a minute?"

"Yes, Doctor?"

"Recently I've been feeling...well...."

"That's good. I thought you were looking a bit peaky the other day there, on your three-score birthday."

"No no no, I've been feeling not too good lately...but...only I couldn't find the right word for it...Debbie, Debbie...could you...er, possibly come over here...for half a second?"

"I'll just finish sterilising these syringes, doctor, prior to re-use. We've been taking so many specimens lately."

"Oh...Nurse...!"

"Yes, Doctor?"

"Y'know I've wondered, if one day...you would ever like...."

"For us to order more disposable syringes, Dr McMoodie? Yes, I think we should. Shall I get the requisition forms from the brrrroom cupboard?"

"Yes, of course, yes, Debbie, no. What I mean is...."

"Contact tracing. Yes, I see what you're driving at, Doctor. We'll eventually have to take swabs from the whole of south west north east Perthshire, shall we not?"

"I know, yes nurse no. There's no other way. Yes. Look nurse, I wonder...Debbie, could you possibly...please...do come over here for just a minute, will you?

"What is it doctor?"

"I didn't want to raise my voice in the surgery."

"No, of course not, doctor."

Debbie, I've been wanting...for a long time...to ask you...if you would ever consider...joining me one evening...for a little... er...tete-a-tete?"

"In the brrrroom cupboard again, you mean?" And give everything there a good going over like last time?"

"No, Debbie, no. What I had in mind was a quiet lunch..."

"Then clean out the dangerous drugs cabinet?"

"Well yes, but no, you're right, we must always...make sure."

> *Oh! what's the use? I need to ask straight out.*
> *All roads lead to Debbie now.*

"Speaking of the...broom cupboard and... dangerous drugs, Debbie, reminds me...."

"Is there something the matter, Doctor?"

"Of something that I've been meaning to ask you for some time, confidentially."

"Yes?"

"Debbie, I became a little concerned, after our...last clean out...as you call it, in the...of the...er...broom cupboard...that day. Tell me, can you recall whether...."

"Yes, it was about a week ago last Tuesday, before the house calls. I had just found that box of your old school rugby shorts. You said you wanted the name tags removed. The cupboard door opened a chink....."

"A small stab of sunlight spilled onto your loose cardigan."

"It was made of dead wool by my mother in order to save money for my nurse's training. She picked it off barbed wire fences and carded it herself."

"Yes indeed, Debbie, yes. But what's more important, what I'm most concerned about, on your behalf...is...."

"Is what, Doctor?"

"After we did...the going over...in the broom cupboard, after we...did you...by any chance...."

"What?"

"Inhale...anything....by chance of course?"

"Oh! Doctor McMoodie, whatever next?"

A large hole opens up in the surgery floor.

THEY ARE BOTH CONSUMED BY FLAMES.

Lights out at La Squala

pungent unguents
for soporific sopranos

CHEDDARDAMERUNG
Twilight of the Goudas

THE OPENING SCENE takes place in the town square in central Parmesania gaily strewn with festive melt-proof bunting. Enter a chorus of salty Rhindmattens in saffron dirndles, carrying raffia baskets of mulled weans. "Now thank we all our Gouda-lings," they sing, while exchanging cheeky comments about country pursuits. They get too merry and lapse into a coma.

Enter Davy Crocket, in aged buckskin, under an assumed name. He removes his 'coon hat, lights his cob pipe, and scoffs a wedge of Worcester, left lying on the inert body of a giant Rhindmatten, then sings the sorrowful air, "I must've made a few bad churns." His tall rifle butt is buttered thickly. Dark-blue darkness falls on the square and Davy backwards down a mouldy manhole.

Brutal Colonel Rod (and his staff) make their ceremonial entrance in three-pea suits and circle the square to clear it. Rod snorts his satisfaction and gnaws on the Worcester left in the floppy fur of Davy Crocket's hat. As the last of his staff leaves he chokes to death singing "Cosi van Stilton."

In the next tents scene, Dipfried plays a shiny tuba on a bar-ren mountain top waiting for his blind cousin's lost half-sister Princess Boneymarone to see, if not wax, to his proposal. But the princess is herself an illicit Rhindmatten and, having nar-rowly escaped the porous calamity of the first scene, reveals her doubts to the audience on the rocky route to the summit. The trenchant aria, "Filth, stuff and nonsense, far out," is sung in her native language and not easily or even usually translated.

The third act, set in a crematorium office that's also the hideout for a headless gang of oiled-up wrestlers, singes our ears with the fiery monologue of the line manageress about poisoning her husband with truffle stuffing from a French Mac-aron factory run by an acting coach. After which, she's playfully squooshed under-foot by a chorus of Cremators in asbestos boots by Hilary Trump.

The overall tone of abject gloom is lifted by the entrance of Dr McFouresome, the harmlessly foul-smelling medical referee, disguised as Sir Davy Crocket. He stubs his toe on a bed pan left out by a ward sister (stunningly played by Nurse Urs from Belten) and, like his unidentified twin, falls backwards over a pile of new mown hay, waiting to be threshed.

The ever playful Cremators scatter the hay like confetti on the newly weds, who, having come down from the mountain by coach and arisen from the sea by conch, make their way to the chapel behind the main entrance to the crematorium car park in thick machine fog.

Where they are joined in a tumultuous final set piece by Rhindmatten's relatives, colourful laundromat attendants and the staff of Colonel Rod. The happy goudalings melt away. No more little red-waxed children here.

Der Friedeggstag von de Closet
Lohengran

SONSIE, SEEMINGLY a below the stairs seamstress of ill repute (but of covert Royal Blood), is excited about her blind date with Flan who, unknowingly, is all too soon to become an aged witch Lohengran's brand new man.

The next scene is set in a hidden shower behind a vestibule where two ardent sailors argue about the unease of continuing their pitiful routines, but are overheard by Flan and Sonsie. Flan appeals to her to take no heed. But she turns to listen to their pleas and, as she does, a huge gap opens between them. Now a chorus of Caramelite nuns emerge from underground, on the horns of a dilemma: after martyrdom, do we wish to be carried to heaven on horseback or on birds' wings? To wit, Mother Superior's touching aria, "Hoof, or the Wings of a Dove?"

Then, in a room at the top of the tower, Lohengran, who has seen it all before, strikes a match in order to find her teeth. She chuckles bitterly as she makes an ominous forecast, in untranslatable writhing couplets derived from faraway tongues: "By this evening there will be a massacre of Queen's Park Rangers by Partick Thistle unless the 'Ger's defence can match the might and meat of the Jag's front four over the ball."

Sonsie, the sailors, and Flan rent a TV and swoon in each other's arms at the end of the match with its devastatingly surprise result.

Lohengran escapes on barge, drawn by swans. However it's a poor likeness, and the whole thing capsizes.

LOHENGRAN AGAIN

LOHENGRAN, since the boat sank, is back in Antwerp. The swans having drawn it as far as they can, put the picture up for auction at the house of TeleRaymond, the media tycoon. In secret, his pagan wife's sister Orotund seeks out Goethefitter, the widely read plumber and now Duke of Manholing, in order to hatch a plot to ascertain the asking price for the artwork. Instead they elope as darkness falls on the monastery garden.

When they get to Kansas, the Girl of the Golden Vest agrees to shelter them on her humble ranch from TeleRaymond's fury. Just then there is a knock on the door and the spotless sheriff Rinse and his posse appear. They are searching for a band of in-laws and food for an orphan's marriage.

Finding Orotund and the Duke of Manholing now nibbling fruit under the floorboards, the posse agree that the pear will do very well. After a long drawn out cleansing scene with Rinse, TeleRaymond is left with another picture on his Hans, the half brother of the auctioneer's right hand man, now stage left.

In the next vivid scene set in Amsterdam, Hans meets the daring young aviator, a chain smoking Flying Dutchman called

Der Faggender Hollander. The two of them sell the drawings and set off round the world on a yacht made of software chips.

Having moused it to the seashore from downtown Dresden, they meet the ghostly reincarnation of Lohengran one moon-lit night, dressed up in a white beard as Santa's mother. She sentences the lovers to a lifetime rounding the Strait but no-one can read her stances because of bad spelling, and the textile crew on board starts to dye laughing.

Migranevitch and the Czar

Migranevitch, the Czar's ageing but ever scornful coquette, tries to seduce Donaldo Bradmanza, the tyrant of Battenpad, by masquerading as a toreador. The Czar smells a rat and thus employs two clowns from Baddodour and Baddudda to put the lovers into a trance by reading them the latest environmental legislation. But their analgesic plan is thwarted by the arrival of the Turkish Armada (with a cargo of accordions keyed for big polkas) under the command of Admiral Whyte-Blanco Bovril, a dusky full-back folksinger from Glenrothes in Scotland's central belt.

With all the aces shuffled in, a bravura future seems in the cards for the labour deck on the Admiral's flagship. But after half time, some bamboozling deliveries leave Donaldo stumped at the finale when rivers overflow just before the whistle.

With the accordions soaked and all the environmental legislation now on hold, Migranevitch and the Czar are reunited and an ancient curse is wrought on Bradmanza by the out-flanked but re-hyphenated Turkish defender from Glenrothes.

The Jackdaw of Eskimonelli

In the first act, the hump backed bully Rudolfo outwits his rivals by wearing a Davy Crocket hat and makes his escape through an open French window into the back garden; pausing for the famous aria "Only the Lawnly".

He sets off for the Frozen North, but hovering over the tundra, is the unspeakable Eskimonelli, step daughter of Loengrinagrin, shamanically transformed into a giant jackdaw. She spots Rudolfo resting on a iceberg in the Bay of Discos and mistakes him, in his Davy Crocket hat, for a small furry mammal. With a shriek (the aria "Nissan Dormouse"), Nelli swoops down like greased lightning and carries Rudolfo off to her sisters who are hiding from a vile tormentor in a launderette under a crevasse, singing, "Only the Laundry".

After a happy landing, the youngest sister slyly asks Rudolfo to say whose voice was the sweetest, hers or Eskimonelli. To which the hump warily replies, "I preferred yours to start with sweetie, but y'know, after a while, Nelli's does crow on you."

A Pilgrim's Christmas

This yuletide opera is set in a sports arena serving as temporary accommodation for a hoard of multinational pilgrims returning from Jerusalem. Customs officers busily search their possessions for concealed weapons.

One of the inspectors, a native Scot, examines a gourd containing milk belonging to a Nicaraguan woman who, in a lively dialogue, explains how she makes these leathery jars in same traditional way as her Mayan forebears. The Scotsman, finding nothing more than the clear liquid left over after removal of the curds, breaks into his seasonal aria when confronted by an inquisitive Major General: "It's a' whey in a Mayan jar."

"And what's that China-man over there doing on a pilgrimage carrying a piece of priceless antique furniture on his back?" asks the Major General which leads to a typical oriental Christmas interlude "Hu Wei in a Ming chair".

Elsewhere, in a crowded gymnasium, a German diplomat from the United Nations, Wolfging Menschauer is holding a press conference, surprisingly interrupted by preparations for a boxing match. He angrily demands to know what's going on, whereupon a squad of dwarf supervisors provide a soothing explanation, to the tune of the familiar carol, "It's a weigh-in, Herr Menschauer."

Finally, the football pitch gets invaded by toxic hares, partially denuded of their fur due to insect infestations. A comic groundsman discovers the first signs of their activities and breaks dismally into a rhythmic yuleish lament: "A Warren, a Mangey Hare."

The End, if you can remember the beginning.

Tarzan Gets Fixed

in Glenrothes

Tarzan's Crisis and Opportunity

DOWN AT THE BIKE SHOP the other day, who should drop in but Tarzan, or a tall lope of a man very like him, in a jungle green suit but with a leopard skin loin cloth and a neatly curled length of liana vine tucked up in a wicker basket. It had to be actually him. I mean anybody with a striking physique, superb tan and rank hair could walk about posing as Tarzan, but would anyone? Certainly not I.

Dotty was just back, looking fresh as ever, from a morning pedal tour of lesser known horse riding stables on the Royal yacht and was first up.

"Are you Tarzan?" she asked brightly and almost curtsied, which set me back a bit, after all we'd been through trying to grow apart together as partners in our mall shop. She would've learned how to back-down and bow in plimmies, bless her, at primary school for the coronation of our dear Queen.

"I am, yes," Tarzan said firmly, "an' I'm lookin' fur a double sided fixed freewheel hub. Ha'e ye got one? Oobutu's driven a freeway through ma jungle, for a new breed of post-colonial poachers. But crisis is opportunity, if ye ken ma meanin'." His BBC central belt accent was despicable. It seemed he'd been misled into being more Central Belt than thou. He probably couldn't tell a cow from a coo.

"I'll have to consult our tech Sandy," Dotty said and vanished through the door to the back room without another word. Did she fancy him or knot? Time might tell, but an automatic smell-check is quicker, I always say.

I sensed by the low pitched rumble in the air and plaster coming off the ceiling that Sandy was on a hummer on the back-room rollers and wouldn't be sitting up on the layback till he'd got to a virtual Auchtermuchty, leaving me alone with Tarzan for a few minutes at the very least.

"How's Jane?" I quipped, "Has she switched to fixed gears as well? It's so modern again. I tried it years ago, but gave up.

Couldn't handle it. Though I did once push a 65. What sprockets you going to have on each side?"

"Jane's fine. We text each other's apps. She still gies liana lessons, wi' both haunds as weel. There's oedema o' the non-weight bearin' side and a weak vibrato in the upper register but otherwise everythin's OK. And wi' a 52 at the front, I'll want 13 and 15 teeth at the rear. Wha's askin'?"

"No kidding? That's a gear of over 80 inches." This was monstrous. Even in wool chinos, you saw he had quads you could eat off. "Does Jane stretch before swings of a morning on a regular basis?" I asked.

"Naw, it's usually the ither way roond. D'ye work here?"

"You could call it that."

"Hae ye got any farings?"

This put his jargon into the Premier League, in my book. It placed him up amongst the Dolomites of cycling science. A Pythagorean and Archimedean combined, he must have been, in a past life. However, the two farings hanging up downstairs were both mine, and anyway I couldn't see what use such aerodynamic efficiency might have up a tree; not that I'm racist, in any shape or form.

Furthermore and fortunately, I suddenly realised the importance of this chance encounter; the opportunities it presented to me, and in a flash, spurning triviality, I blurted out: "Tarzey?"

"Aye?" he replied, evenly.

I hesitated. "Do you mind if I call you Tarzey?".

"Ah would much prefer Tarzan. It's mair dignified a' roond."

"Fair enough. Straight up. OK."

"Please go oan."

He was beginning to sound like an ambassador in a refugee camp, less au natural by the minute.

I went for it.

"I have tug-boat thighs like you, and some elephant-calling training to boot, but can't get most girls to take me seriously. A

44

spot-on sports writer said this was due to upper body dysmorphia. Could...Could you...possibly get Jane to give me some liana lessons...er...discretely? Tell her I won't even smoke, except in breaks between any long swings out front, just like on training runs with the mall squad."

His eyes narrowed with suspicion, and at this precise moment Dotty came back through the door. She'd done a quick stoker's turn on Sandy's tandem rollers, God bless her.

Bells suddenly chimed, but it was only Tarzan knocking over the display cabinet for urban touring accessories, as he swung round to face her. Nevertheless, something certainly sinister seemed afoot now, if not already amiss.

Were we each to become the other's phantom amanuensis (or is it woman anamusis?) in an eternal ivy-strewn amorous quadrangle of mistaken identity? I sneezed loudly and wrung my hands, kneeding a dictionary vigorously to sort out the meaning of all this, the how and why. But there was no entry under either category. Nor was there any meaning given for most of our urban touring accessories for that matter.

Learning Liana. The Basics. Tarzan's Jungle Clearing Gearing

ME AND JANE got on great with the liana lessons. How complicated gearing up for trans-tree swinging really is came as a surprise. Firstly I learned, the working length of the liana vine is critical and must be expressed in English inches only. Greater Gaelic means greater between-tree mileage, and bare feet will painfully scrape the overgrown undergrowth with the swing's lowest maximum, unless the abdominal musculature's up to scratch to hoist them clear.

On the other hand, the boot's on the other foot when you're hanging on to too short a swing in the middle of a smouldering forest clearing with no shrill to speak of. De-mounting is not an option ever, between jumps on a short length; and fixed swing systems are obviously out. So what then is the answer?

Tarzan's adjustable "liana-flex": made from spirally twisted strands of the finest shredded liana impregnated with cork bark for extra friction.

Loops of liana-flex are then coiled round hooped rubber pulleys situated in the micro-canopy above. These reduce friction, so it all balances out. When the dangling (or free swing length) is found wanting, the appropriate number of extra turns required for clearance can be calculated on a hand held turbo-watch. And, that's not all. Utilising an intrinsic spring loaded device, the same is true in vice-versa. Dental options will be on hand for those still having any.

Friction has to be fully balanced, of course too. Otherwise, the roughened skeins of cork bark deliberately woven into the liana-flex will eventually cut through the branch you're swinging from, with you and your Jane winding up in a horrendous snake pit, thereby increasing friction once more in an endless cycle.

TARZAN TAKE THE HIGH ROAD

BACK AT THE BIKE SHOP after my first term at Janey's place on the Congo, my deltoids were looking a lot batter, at least on the spelling side, and I was ready for more foundation training runs with Dotty on the old Ephgrave with its narrow fenders.

Her pestilential mother had been brought in to tape up the urban accessories cabinet and keep an eye on Dotty and Tarzan, after Sandy rashly agreed to Tarzan's idea of rigging up a sauna for the racing squad in the attic beside the cold water tank, with a plunge to follow up. Nothing cheap about Sandy. And Tarzan could dress more naturally in this working environment, though having to crouch the whole time in the limited space available under the roof put the tin lid on his liana research, in Scotland's tight central belt at any rate.

"Ah'm no King Kong," Big T said proudly. His hair remained long and rank in Glenrothes; even with, or maybe because of, all the soaking it got in the sauna. Though with Egg-roll Eddie and Dave Dave out of the racing squad due to speech impediments, only Tarzan and Dotty used the sauna regularly, or so said Dotty's mouthy mother.

So, back home again from another trapezius testing session with Janey on the "ropes" in central Africa, I went upstairs to meet the squad. The intermittent cough and spit coming from the boiler nearby drowned my naked footsteps, and clouds of steam obscured my entrance. Tarzan, looking eerily magnificent in a Goratox "vapour-lock" spotted loin cloth and Dotty (herself resembling a stunning bespoke oil painting from a bygone era) were in earnest conversation and oblivious to all else.

"Tarz?" she said, and my heart froze, suspended, in spite of the hot steam everywhere. Why had I never been accorded this level of intimacy during aeons of cycle camping in the Central Belt with her?

I could just make out the new Brompton folding bicycles neatly parked beside them both, as if they'd just been delivered of identical twins. Titanium of course being rustproof.

"Tarz?" she continued.

"Yes, Dot." The way they both spoke to the other was utterly nauseating, as if each was oiling the other's chain at the same time.

"Tarz, tell me something....about your mother. You hardly ever speak about her."

I stopped flapping my towel to attract attention and paused for a little to think about the ramifications of this request myself. Tired, partially wrapped and awkwardly crouched in a cramped sauna vestibule, I was quite glad she wasn't asking me about my own mother just then.

I could hear Tarzan holding his breath.

"Tarz, please don't ignore me like this. It's so insulting. I feel excluded."

He wasn't ignoring her. He'd just stopped breathing, that's all. Anyone could see that, even in a steam filled sauna. And no wonder.

"You're sulking again, what have I done, Tarzie? Please."

Silence. Though breathing had resumed, albeit stertuitously, or stortorously. Whatever, it sounded like the heavy irregular snoring said to precede the onset of apoplexy. Yet, I was rooted to the spot and could not go forward.

Silence.

"Tarz?"

"Yes Dot, ah hear ye."

"Thank you."

"Ah wis jus' thinkin', sweet one, why don't we gang doon-stairs and have yin o' those bonny...what d' ye call 'em...welched rabbits...that ah've grown sae fond of' these days. Aw` lassie, y'er a right sonsie wee...."

Dotty suddenly exploded then into a huge flaring rage and stormed out, taking her neatly folded Brompton with her.

But as she swung it hurriedly round to leave, she banged the folding hinge into one of my outstretched legs, unaware of my presence in the enveloping steam, and slicing my thigh. My feet began to feel numb and tingly due to blood loss. Dotty's dear voice echoed round the soft wet walls of the sauna. Words poured out of her in a blur...the result of years and years of true tenderness frustrated, it has to be said, by the effect of the large flange hubs on the old Ephgrave; long deemed unsuitable for a woman with one leg shorter than the other. But now, with the technical malarkey no longer between us, her loving words tumbled forth in a surging torrent.

"Oh," she said, "There you are, Les. What a surprise you gave me and what in god's name are you're doing here? Mum said you were on intensive training in a diminishing tropical rain forest. Here, that gash looks nasty, we'd better get it looked at. I can take you to the emergency room in the trailer Sandy fettled up for Eddie's wedding. Gosh you do look pale, are you feeling poorly? We could have a quick brew up before we go, and there's some spare porkers under the back seat of the Cortina, do you remember? Here...I think we should phone for an ambulance right away. I'll get...Tarzan!!"

She shouted for him through the steam, in vain because but he was already gone, cycling his now unfolded Brompton across the sky as if he were in a re-make of *ET* and leaving a deftly twisted length of new issue liana-flex dangling straight upwards out a sash window that he'd forcibly smashed. This tied everything up neatly, to an end, as the sauna caught fire soon after,

Maybe as well as a Pythagorist, he'd also been Oahatma Ghandi in a past life. Hence the loin cloth dependency syndrome and astonishing rope tricks. He certainly had fixed wheel gearing, pacifism, and charisma down to a fine art, even without the advantage of a convincing local patois.

But, it turned out, it was a humble welsh rabbit ultimately that torpedoed his idea of a secluded retirement and rehab in Glenrothes with my Dotty.

Deirdre of the Pillows

Tawdry tales &

fashionable innuendo

from below the Central Belt

LADY TWOBRAS
DORNOCHER'S VERSION

WHO'S WHO IN LOCH GRIDLOCH

BRAD	prosperous owner of a huge dock
DEIRDRE	window cleaner bint
TRACEY	scurf dealer's moll
NIETZSCHE	morbid non-identical twin
CLINT	scum-bag's runner
NOBBIE	front row forward with hard tackle and divergent squint
STACEY	statuesque waitress about to take Holy Orders
LACEIGH	single minded car wash attendant with neat double breasted jacket

THE STORY SO FAR

ONCE UPON A TIME there was Brad & Stacey. They first ran into Clint & Tracey at a walk-in clinic for the legless where Nietzsche was on an attachment. Brad kept his smack at his huge dock in between off-the-cuff voyages round the Horn with Stacy and his lively live-in accountant and mother-of-two Deirdre, who also had a warm flat of her own nearby.

One day, with an hour before the children needed fetching from the car wash, Deirdre invited everyone round for snacks in her new-wave wireless split-level loungette. Luckily, Brad had just finished cleaning the windows and had the folding beds out by the time they all arrived. In no time they were all hard at it discussing the pros and cons of Nietzsche's sardonic wrath when Nobbie looked in with lingerie and frozen butter which he laughingly put in the micro-wave, turned out the lights and lazily drew the curtains.

Nietzsche's Rash Assumption

"**The earth** must have moved," Deirdre pondered the following morning, "The slats of the venetian blinds have gone diagonal." She soon realized this was due to the collapse of the folding bed. Rolling over Brad and Nobbie, she got up and searched around for her high heels which she eventually found in the butter.

Suddenly there was a knock on the door. She opened it to Laceigh in a sawn off mini-kilt and split crutch bra calling by.

"I just happened to be in the area so I thought I'd drop in and, um, read the...um books," she quipped.

"You don't need a split-clutch bra to read books, surely," Nobbie whispered under his breath.

"I suppose you'll help Clint choose hymns for the wedding also," chimed in Deirdre, pulling on her foundation silk jersey half-slip. "Being a big girl, you'll probably plump for "Victor after Hard Won Day." They all laughed heartily at this, then got up and down to a casual breakfast.

Laceigh looked round the tawdry scene, her red curly hair blazing naturally. "What was it last night then? A glee-some threesome, or an awesome foursome?"

"We could have a pic 'n' mix'em six-em, right now, if you'd like," lisped Tracey, through a mouth full of baguette, "after you've done the books that is. If only you could get Nietzsche to join in once again. What's with him these days, Laceigh?"

"His mother just told him that a third non-identical twin was born the day after him and his mute sister, who failed to thrive. Nietzsche says it must have been the after-birth but his mother insisted it had legs. At least partly so. So now poor Friedrich's got it into his head that he's not a real twin after all, but some kind of freak non-identical tri-placenta. It could explain the ugly spot he sometimes has on his front. He always attributed it to the beatings he got in the nursery."

"I always blamed his mother. Right from the beginning," blurted Clint. Several others nodded.

"Now don't you start. What do any of you know about it?"

"Getting him to do the lavvy rims throughout the house with torn out pages of his remaindered *Tractors*, a reference work about mixed farming in the central belt."

"Making him scrape the scum off his own bath. No wonder," added Deidre, half frowning from a failed botox.

"Oh, get on track, all of you. I'm going," cried Laceigh heartily. And, haughtily drawing up the ruched sleeves of her stylish off-the-shoulder slit blouson, she left right away.

Rose fizz with the Newly Weds

"How would you like your steak this morning, Clint?" murmured Laceigh, half into a wholesome little lycra frock and pinnie two-piece.

"Oh...in-between," Clint replied, browsing a wine list and model web-site, legs akimbo in gutted pink Y-fronts .

"In between whom, Tracey and Stacey? A bit early in the day, isn't it, for a three coarse meal?"

"Now don't keep going on about the old days," Clint averred. "You know perfectly well all that came to an end once Tracey and Nietzsche took up Gestalt down at the car wash. And anyway I'm not really all that hungry. Here, what do you think of this Rose?"

"Never heard of her."

"Impressive pungent strawberry and bramble aromas; well balanced with succulent ripe fruits."

"She'll be a modern woman, I dare say she has."

"It's the fizz, for after, silly."

"Would you like my fizz to taste like that after? I'll get some. What should I serve it with? Would a wet blouse be all right?"

"It says here you can quaff it on its own while on one of these latest cardio-trainers."

"Not my latest one, I shouldn't think. He got a gammy leg

from maintaining aerobic thresholds with Deirdre all last weekend at the hydro."

Suddenly once more there were footsteps at the door. It was Nobbie, in a spiffing set of tight cotton slacks and another pack of butter.

"I brought it for Nietzsche," Nobbie panted breathlessly, "knowing how much it helped him with his spot the last time."

"But Nietzsche goes down to the car-wash with Tracey on Mondays, ever since the wedding...You must know that. What are you thinking off, Nobbie, have you gone mad?" Clint muttered fiercely. "Stop banging on the door. Laceigh's still undressed. We're having egg rolls," he added, uncertainly.

"You're just trying to hide him from me. Me and Stacey. Aren't you? I bet the whole gang of you are in there now. Why are you...."

"Nobbie, you're off your head mate. Too much bunny boiling, old son. Deirdre and Brad went on a world tour after her horse hit a pylon and got electrocuted. Stacey's a waitress in Glenrothes and thinking of taking Holy Orders. Go home and get your blood tested, Nobbie. Lace and me, we're through with all this malarkey and hoping to get married ourselves all too soon in the near future."

A Tangled Web of Whited Sepulchres

Deirdre and Tracey, looking fair tuckered out, were having a friendly chat one evening just after Clint left for night shift. It had been one in and one out the front door for Tracey and Clint for weeks now that they were both working to pay off the dry cleaners after the wedding.

"I just thought I'd pop by on my way to the um Forensic Dentistry class," Deirdre said, adding helpfully, "and I wanted to say sorry for Nobbie's part in the balls up of the seating plan at the chapel. Putting the car wash attendants in the second row in matching double breasted blazers said the wrong thing," she added, undoing the top button of a polo style chamois leather chemise, and gently stroking her neck.

"Phew" she went on, "there's an interesting smell around here. Got anyone in? Are these yours?" she enquired, pointing to a pair of men's suspenders caught on the handle of the kitchen door.

"No, they're Clint's."

"The buckles have got red crosses on them. Has he taken up First Aid? And who's whose left all these screwed up bits of paper lying around?" Deirdre said, raising an eyebrow with difficulty.

"It's just rough notes, for a sexy sort of story we've been thinking of."

"Only thinking of? After a week's holy matrimony? Sound interesting. I'd better read one."

"No, don't." Tracey grabbed a ball of paper from Deirdre's hand, but Deirdre got hold of another. Soon they were having a playful tussle on the deep shag pile of the front hall carpet.

"'Truly, with one bestial howl, I will blast out the contents of all philosophically whited sepulchres and jeer at them with sardonic wrath,'" Deirdre read out loud, "Here, wait a minute, this is Nietzsche's sort of stuff, and in his own handwriting as well. You've been seeing to him again haven't you, Tracey? On Clint's nightshift. No wonder you're looking so tuckered out."

"It's his rash, Deirdre, I promise. Shouting abusive texts at me while I strangle the poor dear is the only thing that keeps it at bay. I never read a word of it myself. I don't even understand it. Don't get me wrong."

"I won't. But what have whited sepulchres got to do with red cross mini-suspenders Tracey?"

"It's what he brings his morbid tracts rolled up in. He doesn't write them on the spot, you know."

"Well obviously not. It would be very painful. Even if he's only got a single one. Well, all I can say is don't let Clint in on this tangled web of whited sepulchres Tracey, wrapped or un-wrapped in suspenders. I must say, that I always found being sardonic with Clint pretty useless, compared with whipping."

"And another thing," Deirdre said, as the flashing light of a passing ambulance illuminated the faint bruise that Tracey was stroking, "I'm noticing how that love bite on your neck has a small area of undamaged skin on the left side, corresponding with an absent lower second incisor, exactly, just like my Nobbie's," she flared. "Have you, Nietzsche and Nobbie, all three of you, been having sardonic threesome sex above the car wash on Clint's nightshift behind my back?"

Tracey blushed to the very roots of her core being, just as Brad came by on a week's leave with Laceigh plus carry-out on one arm and Stacey, done up as a nun, on the other.

ELECTRIC ASSIST. CLINT'S LAST RIDE

"WHERE'S NOBBIE?" asked Clint one day many years later, clad in crushed maroon corduroy chinos, relaxing with some of the others in the saloon bar of what had once been a prosperous car wash before it was shut down by Health and Safety.

"Dunno," replied Laceigh listlessly, due to sleeping sickness caught at the Olympics. "The last I heard he was in relapse with his malaria, crippled with arthritis, and needing...injections... of fresh blood...into his brain," she moaned, falling over and frothing at the mouth as discreetly as ever.

The re-union had gone really well so far. In spite of the new lift at the hydro annexe only taking two of the friends' wheel chairs at a time.

"Shame. I liked him, in spite of his divergent squint." Did you two..." Clint said, turning to Tracey and Stacey, "ever, er break it off with Nietzsche, so to speak?

"Didn't have to", cut in Stacey, in no way held back by her new leg, "Accidental death. Expostulating about something or other with nothing on in a colourful brothel. Madame dropped a plate of lamb chops down his ear trumpet. Went downhill rapidly. At the end he had to stay awake all day in order to go to sleep. Did I hear you were in traction, Brad? "

"Since the pace-maker in my haemorrhoid caved in, yes."

"I'm the same. That ties us up together again," said Deirdre.

"It was the annihilating power of his exuberance, that did for Freidreich in the end," Stacey said, "I told him."

"I was always telling him," lisped Tracey through the froth. "Exuberance, Friedrich is no way to clear a path towards a freer expression of your Anti-Moral Truths," I'd say, "Even down at the car wash."

"Freidrich loved that car wash, didn't he? Never a one for the open countryside."

"No. You couldn't have called him an ecological Neitzche."

"All those years ago," they all muttered, manoevering their electric wheel chairs closer together. "Those Anti-Moral Truths of his were something else," wheezed Brad.

"I'll say," they all agreed, whispering softly now so as not to say too much in one breath. "That's probably why he took up Gestalt down at the car wash in the first place."

"Not the double breasted blazers of the attendants at all then?"

"Apparently not."

"Madame at the brothel wouldn' t hear of it. His Anti-moral Truths."

"Neither could he. He preferred to say, 'What doesn't kill you makes you stronger.' He wanted it on his tombstone. And that was when the lamb chops fell down his ear trumpet."

Tracey sighed sentimentally, "I remember him saying once, as I was doing his spot, 'In heaven all the interesting people will be missing.'"

"D'you think that applies to us?" asked Deirdre in a very soft voice.

"What was that, Deirdre?" they said, but she was distracted

57

by some jerking of the controls of her electric chair.

"Deirdre?...Speak up!" and they all moved their chairs even closer together, cupping their ears with their free hands.

Just then Deirdre's wheelchair lunged forwards completely out of control and dragged the others' with her, all tangled up together, towards an open set of French windows which led onto a flimsy balcony above an abandoned building site, umpteen stories below.

Where, once upon a time, there had been a thriving car wash with single minded attendants in ample double breasted blazers. The ruins of which were about to bring the curtain down on Deirdre, Clint, Tracey, Brad, Lacey, Nobbie, Stacey, Nietzsche's Anti-Moral Truths and the whole bang shoot.

The Merry Wives of Santa

a seasonal extravaganza

"...fuses the dialectic of virtually every known form of great dramatic play ever written with the true spirit of Xmas...."
Tennessee Ernie Datsun in the BOG O' BADBREATH BUGLE

DRAMATIS PERSONNAY

CYNTHIA (aka Agatha)...........................Australian Tennis Star
CHARLES...ditto
HENRY V (disguised as Brad).......................Rhyming monarch
INSPECTOR DAWSON WINDOWS.........Defective detective
PUCK...Constipated sprite
BRECHT...Alienated playwright
Mrs BRECHT...Inn keeper
SANTA CLOSIDES..White bearded oaf
CLOSETLADES, KNOTHOLES, STEPASIDES......Santa's 3 wives
PRINCESS DEMENTIA.................................An exotic being
THE NAWAB OF STANGLEABANGHA...........................Ditto

(The action takes place in Australia, Berlin, in Glasgow Central Station and a Room at the Inn)

Scene 1

A DRAWING ROOM WITH FRENCH WINDOWS OPENING ONTO A FIELD OF THE CLOTH OF GOLD OVERLOOKING THE SEA IN AUSTRALIA. SOUNDS OF A CLOSE TENNIS MATCH.

CYNTHIA   How can we have a mystery without a victim?

CHARLES   We're all created victims, Agatha.

CYNTHIA   Is that why you always wear black corduroy trousers, Henry?

CHARLES   No, it's because I'm in mourning for a past life.

CYNTHIA   It's the waiting I can't stand, for those red sails in the sunset, to bring my fate to me.

CHARLES   How lovely. But hark ! Is that a tennis ball I hear exploding?

ENTER A CALEDONIAN PRIMARY SCHOOL CHILDREN CHORUS DRESSED AS SHEEP

SHEEP   We're awa tae Bethlem too-oo-oon. We're awa tae Bethlem too-oo-oon.

HENRY V   And so child sheep sought Charles and Cynthia's
            pardon by singing carols in their neat back
            garden. But Hark! 'tis Sir Furren Sealance.
            Back from a hazardous cruise. What tidings
            bring you from the China seas. What news?

Scene 2
LATER THAT EVENING IN ANOTHER GARDEN IN BERLIN, INSPECTOR
DAWSON WINDOWS IS QUESTIONING THE ENTIRE WEEKEND HOUSE
PARTY AFTER A FOSSILIZED HUMAN BEING WAS FOUND ON A SHELF IN
THE LIBRARY. SOUNDS OF ANGRY SEAMEN OUTSIDE IN THE STREET.

WINDOWS   Miss Bellwearing, where were you on the night
            in question, when Cain betrayed Abel?

BELLWEARING With the vicar, my brother-in-law. He was
            the hind legs of our pantomime Rudolph.

WINDOWS   Indeed? Then how could he possibly have known
            the colour of Cynthia's wallet in the library if he
            was playing the rear end of a reindeer in the
            servants' quarters?

ALLIED SEAMEN   Strike!!Strike!! Strike!!
(OFF-STAGE)   Boots!! Boots!! Boots!!
BELLWEARING Because the vicar had given it to her in the first
            place, as a pre-Christmas present.

BRECHT   Panto is dead!! Drab costumes!!
(OFF-STAGE)   Back projection!! Vivid lighting!!
BELLWEARING We'd all just got back from dinner in Eden
            and were about to taxi to the theatre.

WINDOWS   But that doesn't explain...God, I can't hear my
            self think. We'd better join the others indoors
            and get more mince pies down the neck.

ALLIED SEAMEN   Dissolve the People!! Elect another!
(OFF-STAGE)

62

Scene 3

GLASGOW CENTRAL STATION. SNOW FALLING. SHOPPERS MILLING ABOUT GROANING UNDER BURDENSOME BAGS OF GIFTS. PRINCESS DEMENTIA AND THE NAWAB OF STRANGLABANGHA LOOK ON IN BEWILDERMENT AND DISBELIEF.

HENRY V   Agatha! Gosh, you're looking fair done in, old scout. Porter! Will you take these bags here, if you please? Far out.

PUCK   I'll put a girdle round the earth. And plummet o'er the moon's. Drink juice that's made of cariboos and smooth albino prunes.

SALESMAN   My son. My lost son.

HE DIES. CORPSE REMOVED BY A CORP OF GIRL GUIDES, DONE UP AS CARPENTER'S WIVES. ENTER THE VIRGIN MARY, WITH OTHER HOUSE GUESTS. ON THE HAND OF SIR BATHDEIS CZERNY, THEY PASS STRIGHT THROUGH TO THE FIRST CLASS COURTESY LOUNGE.

DEMENTIA   But Strangleabangha, this altercation is idle. In this nauseating charade you have executed the precepts of your overbearers' seasonal requests and yet your feelings towards me have under gone a complete volte face. Why?

ENTER GOD. HE BLOWS A WHISTLE, MAKING FITTING GESTURES, AND THE PASSENGERS, INCLUDING THE NAWAB, JUST MANAGE TO CRAM THEMSELVES INTO THE OVERHEATED SECOND CLASS CARRIAGES BEFORE THE TRAIN DEPARTS. BRECHT ASSUMES FALSE WHITE BEARD AND EMBRACES PRINCESS DEMENTIA WARMLY.

Scene 4

A ROOM AT THE INN. MOUNTED OX AND ASSES HEADS JUT OUT FROM THE WALLS. AN ASSAULT RIFLE HANGS ABOVE THE FIREPLACE. A GIGANTIC TURKEY ON THE TABLE.

BRECHT   I am a resident in the suburbs of the metropolis and my vixen wife doesn't understand me. Here she comes now. I will tell her some pretty

| | fable that will set me free to enjoy horn willed Princess Dementia. Ha there, wife. I'm troubled by dreams and must consult a skilled therapist. I suggest Mrs Lu Poo Few. |
| MRS BRECHT | You're talking complete rubbish, Brecht. Dreams proceed from Organic Disturbance. Get your arse down to a proper clinic and then help me stuff this turkey for the orphans. It's enormous. |

CLOUDS OF RUBBLE SPURT FROM THE FIREPLACE. DOWN THE CHIMNEY COME THE MERRY WIVES OF SANTA DRESSED AS A CHORUS OF CLASSIC GREEK COMEDIENNES BUT WEARING POINTED RED HATS, FALSE WHITE BEARDS, AND FLAUNTING KITSCH WEDDING RINGS.

CLOSETLADES	Where's Santa? Why hasn't he joint our humerus party? Ha ha.
STEPASIDES	Chopping physic probably. Making mattock war on manic knotholes. He He He
KNOTHOLES	Why single me out? Curry that vortex!! What have I done? Flout shame!! The sun's a cigar!! Look! Santa seems stuck up the chimney. Let's investigate. (ALL TOGETHER) Santa where are you?
SANTA	(VOICE OFF, UP CHIMNEY) I'm up here. Chimney caved in on me. Rudolph must have kicked it in when we landed. Spot of dry rot probably too. The chimney that is. Ho Ho. Terribly sorry. The orphans'll have to do without me. Ho.

THEY ALL REPAIR OFF-STAGE TO THE KITCHEN. HYSTERICAL LAUGHTER. MRS BRECHT TAKES DOWN THE RIFLE AND JOINS THEM. SOUNDS OF GUNFIRE. MRS BRECHT RE-ENTERS. HAIR AWRY, RIFLE SMOKING, AND STARTS STUFFING THE TURKEY BUT LOSES INTEREST, YAWNS, SLOWLY FALLS ASLEEP OVER THE TURKEY AS IF IT WERE A PILLOW. ENTER INSPECTOR DAWSON WINDOWS. HE SNIFFS AROUND AND EXAMINES THIS AND THAT MINUTELY WITH A MAGNIFYING GLASS, TAKING NOTES AS HE DOES SO. HE IS STARTLED TO DISCOVER THE INERT MRS. BRECHT. WHISPS OF

SMOKE ISSUE FROM THE KITCHEN DOOR. HE GOES INTO THE KITCHEN
AND COMES BACK OUT IMMEDIATELY AND WAKES UP MRS. BRECHT.

WINDOWS The game's up missus. There's a poet and three
white bearded babes in there, all dead on the
floor and here's the smoking gun. This is an open
and shut case if ever I saw one and I must ask you
to accompany me to police headquarters. And
don't tell me you used it to kill the turkey.

HE CLAMPS ONE END OF A HANDCUFF ON HER WRIST AND THE OTHER
ON HIS. SHE RESISTS BEING TAKEN AWAY.

MRS BRECHT I won't inspector, but when you hear the whole-
WINDOWS Come along now. None of your stories.
MRS BRECHT Berthold and his bourgeois babes just had to go.
WINDOWS Come along now.
MRS BRECHT It was a metaphor, a metaphor we can do
without in the modern age.
WINDOWS Look you just come along with me. And don't
give me any more of your metaphors.

MRS BRECHT STANDS HER GROUND AND SINGS THE EPILOGUE DIRECTLY
TO THE AUDIENCE.

*O **Christ**mas O **Christ**mas/ that **word** gets to my **bones**/
All that **pho**ney **wor**ship in 2.5 family **homes**/
And that **fat** old **guy** and his **rein**deer/ some furry **red**
toy **mon**gering **gno**me/ skating about the **sky**
down chimneys of **plated sto**ne. With that **jing** jing **jing**ling
nonsense about a **fat**her deranged in **Rome**/ whose
gifts are **just** entice**ments** to **over**do the **growth** hor**mone**/
And the **Christ**mas **tur**keys look **ner**vously
about what they call **flesh** and **bone**/
They know too **hon**estly who's **din**ner and who is **done**.*

BRECHT Maybe they'll stage this after I'm dead.

Scallywag the Terrible

True tales of an undersized runt's hair-raising scrapes

According to SIROPAN FIGGS

The Curse of Hazel's Mum

"Woof," said Scally, wagging his tail hopefully, as he and Hazel's mum passed the butcher's shop on the way to collect Hazel from school. "Woof, Woof Woof," he added, veering towards a nearby lamp post where there were unmistakeable signs that Nettie, a poodle from the new flats, had passed this way only minutes before...leaving a message for him.

Scally pulled up so suddenly at the lampost to leave his reply that Hazel's mum, hanging onto the lead, was brought to an abrupt halt and, lurching backwards, dropped her shopping bag...which contained the cake she'd just bought for Hazel's birthday sleep-over with her best pals Lucie and Trixie that very night.

"Hannibal!" she shrieked (for this was Scally's real name, on the tag attached to his collar when they found him, a runt abandoned on a rubbish heap out of town. "Hannibal! Look what you've done. You mustn't just stop like that any time you want and refuse to go on. Hazel's cake will be ruined. Uuugh. She opened the box and the cake inside was half squashed. "You are really such a scallywag. You've got to learn!" she said trying to tug him away.

"It'll be all right, Mum," a sweet voice said from behind her as Hazel and the girls, out of school early with art cancelled, came up with their Mums. "We'd already decided we want to make cup cakes of our own tonight anyway if that's alright."

The other mums all nodded.

And while the necessary ingredients were eagerly discussed, Scally found himself face to face with a half torn shopping bag from which protruded crushed fragments of the best smelling cream cake he'd ever seen. Not unnaturally for a Jack Russell / Airedale cross with an Imperial pedigree on one side, Scally thought that this feast, conveniently served up at nose height, was his dinner, even though it was a bit unusual, even with the human race, to get pudding before the main course.

He was well into what he regarded as rightful booty before the other Mums saw what was going on and started giggling.

"Hannibal. You naughty dog," blurted Hazel's mum.

"He's not" cried Hazel.

"He's got to be trained. Just like you and me."

Trained for what, thought Mrs Cleaverly, one of the mums. "Our dog Nettie would have done the same, wouldn't she, Trix?"

"There's plenty left. We can make it into smaller little cup cakes. It'll add to the fun."

"But he's dribbled all over it".

"Only a small bit. We can cut that half off and use the rest."

"And poke some glacé cherries into the cream," chimed in Lucie.

"OK yes, all right. Then we'll just chuck the remains."

"Might as well give then to Scally."

"It'll just make him sick."

"It'll put him to sleep."

Give him the whole lot then, thought Hazel's mum, and with the glacé cherries in it as well, he might never wake up.

Suddenly out of nowhere a clap of thunder followed a bolt of lightning and rain began bucketing down. Scally, like his imperial namesake, never made the mistake of confusing association with causation. He simply loved sleep-overs, and wagged his tail hopefully.

SCALLY AND NETTY ON THE LOOKOUT.

"HULLO THERE, NETTIE. I got your message. It's so nice up here behind this builder's dump. Good view. Out of the wind."

"Have a gnaw at the other end this bone? What's up at the sleep-over?"

"I won't, thanks. Just now anyway. Hazel's Dad got a nose-bleed half way through the puppet show. Put the kibosh on the whole thing. Feeling a bit queezy myself, as a matter of fact. Rather overdid the cake somewhat."

"I heard that Trixie's dad got back from work looking a bit peely-wallie himself. Look Scall, something's up. All the birds say so. And the horses. Even the rats...Something strange is going on round here. We may have to intervene in some way."

"Well, no-one's getting art classes restored to Primary 5, Nettie."

"Maybe not. But don't forget the dog is god spelt backwards."

"Thanks for reminding me. I'm always surprised this isn't more widely known."

"Much better that way. No-one suspects our influence on human behaviour."

"Yes, they treat us like dogs."

"Much better that way for us."

"But the food's not as good as it was before domestication, I always say."

"I've often heard you. Your greed is ridiculously comic, but that's what I like. You're such a skallywag, Scally."

"You try being a runt Jack Russell with short legs and an Airedale's long hairy pelt, dragging along the ground all day."

"I can't imagine how your Mum and Dad ever conceived you. But your hair makes you so cuddly, Scall. It's why you get on well with children...You'd be better with grown-ups if you didn't dribble so badly."

"It runs in the family. You Poodles are so picky. Where does your lot come from? "

"Ancient Egypt. Believe it or not, we Poodles are descended from wild Jackals, who, half dressed up as humans, took the Pharaohs for their last walk, down to the river, when it was time for them to die. No refusals. No turning back."

"Mmm...Hazel's dad doesn't take me out at all these days. And with her mum, it's funny how often we get thunder, lightening, and a downpour so we have to cut it short. What a temper that woman has. Do the dickie birds think there's going to be a volcano or something? They can often tell in advance."

"They say we animals have to watch and wait. I thought I ought to tell you".

"Too right. We're all in this together. Even those bloody rats. God, how I hate them. They've got to be stopped. They get everywhere, they'll eat anything. They've got no taste"

They're highly intelligent, Scall, let them be. There's a fox in the empty flats below us that keeps them in check."

"Too damn clever for their own bloody good."

"Rats really get you going, don't they, Scally.? And many would find 'Dickie Birds' a species abusive term as well."

"I'd do more rat holes myself if my long pelt didn't get all clogged up with mud. It makes me look ridiculous. I've got my pride."

"But Hazel loves giving you a bath."

"Yes. You know, I really do approve of that girl."

"More than me?"

"Now don't you start. That's the kind of thing the girls will be blathering on about down at the sleep-over."

You'd better be getting back then, Scall. Before the glacé cherries put you to sleep or Hazel's dad gets another nose bleed. It's not blather by the way. It's the way young girls rehearse reality. Catch you later."

"Hopefully, yes."

Grandad's Pink Mouse Saves the Day

"What happened next?" asked Chief Inspector Archer.

Before Hazel could reply, a loud banging, thumping and scraping noise disturbed the back door. Archer, taking no chances, was up out of his seat in a flash.

"It'll be Hannibal," said Hazel's dad, "we'd better let him in."

"Hannibal?" Has the whole family gone mad? Are traces of blood on the man's dressing gown collar? Archer wondered

"It's Hazel's dog," mum added helpfully. "He must have just

woken up. Give him his biscuits and a squeaky bone and he'll not bother us. Will you?" she went on, opening the door. "You sit on your nice rug, Hannibal, will you? I've cleaned it. Gooood dog. He's getting better. Yes, Inspector. Well, what happened next was that...Hazel, I think, you'd better...carry on from where you left off."

"Well," gasped Hazel, "We'd just got the sleeping bags out and I was speaking to Lucie with my back to Trix about why she was so angry that Elspeth no longer spoke to her at break after the argument between me and Kay at reception last week when Trixie got really upset feeling left out and started to cry saying it was because...."

"Try and stick to the point darling. Inspector has a lot to do!"

"But this is the point! Trixie said she was being ignored because she and her mum had only just recently moved in to the neighborhood and Lucie said no it wasn't that at all and I said the same but Trixie cried and cried and cried and buried herself right down at the bottom of her bag. Then we heard this terrific scream and Trixie jumped out of her bag holding a wet gungy thing in her hand. Look, this proves it! Which one of you's put this filthy soggy mess in my sleeping bag?"

It was Grandad's mouse, all ripped apart and smeared with chocolate like....

"What a frightful shock," whispered Archer sympathetically. He'd seen a thing or two in the engine room of the Royal Navy.

"Yes. It was Grandad's birthday present. At first I thought a mouse was a bit babyish for birthday present but as granddad had made it himself...."

"Made the mouse himself?" queried the Inspector worriedly, not being a creationist. "What...has this got to do with it?"

Hazels's mum felt it was time to cut to the chase and went on soothingly, "Granpa, my husband's father that is, had made a mouse out of one of his socks, a pink one, and not taking much interest in it at the time, Hazel got on with opening all her other presents and the mouse must have got buried beneath all that wrapping paper. And forgotten about."

"Quite," rallied the Inspector, "but how...how...how does this connect with finding someone trying to break into your car last night?" He must have missed a clue here somewhere.

"This is where Hannibal comes in," said Hazel, fierce pride glinting in her eyes.

"Woof," barked Hannibal. Squeaky bones were beneath his dignity. But, after last night's scrapes, biscuits would do for now. He wagged his tail thoughtfully and hopefully.

"Naturally", Hazel's Mum continued, "I rushed in when I heard Trixie's scream and we soon realised that it was Hannibal who must have found the mouse abandoned under the other presents' wrapping paper and chewed it up."

"And then, having first demolished the remains of the chocolate cake," Hazel added, "he squirreled the mouse away in a sleeping bag for safe keeping, to return to it later."

"And play around with its remains like it was a real rat in a hole," added Hazel's dad.

"Don't..." gasped Hazel.

Hazel's mum went on, "Trixie was having hysterics. So we locked Hannibal outside with his mangled mouse for the rest of the night, Naughty Hannibal. He must've finally been sick, right beside the car, and that's what the thief slid on and fell over. He fell so heavily that his shout woke us all up, including Hannibal."

"Who flew at him like a brick in a hearth rug," Hazel's dad continued. "Bit of a star this dog. Just as well," he added darkly. "There was Top Secret stuff from the factory on a USB left in the glove compartment. My mistake, Inspector."

"I heard," said Scally to Nettie that evening up at the dump, "that this USB contained data about a gas leak at the factory slowly poisoning people who worked near it. Like your Trixie's dad and my Hazel's, who were trying to prevent news getting out about it till more about the poisoning was known. Gagging on that pink mouse and the chocolate cake plus those glacé cherries saved their bacon."

"Bacon?"

"A tastey type of roast piglet that you and your vegetarian family won't know about. Treat it as a metaphor for something highly valued. Like a brick in a hearth rug, like...."

"Some folk'll eat anything. But nobody gets to call you a naughty dog again, Scall," murmured Nettie with a friendly smile. "And they'll just have to put up with your dribbling from now on."

"About time", said Hannibal , feeling equally friendly, and a touch heroic, and wagging his tail so thoughtfully.

Nettie and Scally to the Rescue

"Scall, I need your help badly. Usual place, round about mid-night. Get yourself plausibly locked out again if you can," said the message left on the dead stump of a new tree planted by the lay-by at the entrance to the Park, and it ran all over the place, making it hard to read. As if one of Nettie's legs hadn't been in good shape at the time of delivery.

"Hannibal, what you growling about?" barked Hazel's mum, "You've never stopped growling since you had your nice jelly. What's wrong? There's nothing wrong with it. I can't think straight. Is it Grandad's violin? I thought as much. Well, we'll just have to try you out on your new cork mat outside. Look, it's a full moon and quite warm too. You can growl happily till you want back in."

"HAAYMIIISH" she howled at her husband, "I'm just taking Hazel to her new dog obedience class, and then the ballet after as usual. The fox hunt's been revived and there's a new master of hounds."

"Nettie, what happened to your leg?" panted Scally, very out of breath, at the dump. He'd come up like a speeding bullet.

"Set on by a bitch in the park, out on my own. Its owner managed to get her off luckily and bundled her efficiently into his van. I got home and pretended it doesn't hurt so's I could

73

get out here tonight but it does, so I must be quick. Scally, I've been trying to get those two new fox cubs out of the empty flats below us and find a safer place for them. Their mum's been killed by the new hunt. I'd got one out into the woods, but on the way back for the other one, that vicious bitch, probably part of the hunt, must have smelt fox on my mouth and went for me. I can't do the other one Scally, I'm too weak. Can you help?"

****

Here's how it happened:
Nettie, Trixie and her mum's flat was right on the edge of town. At the back of the block was undeveloped ground, including a small wild wood. One day, months before, coming back from a walk, they spotted a fox in the woods and Trixie suggested they get some scraps from the butcher's and leave them out for her. Which they did, putting them in the same place each time, out of harm's way inside a rotten old tree. Weeks later, Trixie and Nettie were out on their own with juicy morsels when they were met by the same fox, holding two cubs in her mouth this time, which she displayed proudly, even thankfully, but also to show that extra supplies would now be needed.

Of course, unknown to the family, it was Nettie who put the idea into Trixie's head to suggest feeding the fox in the first place, knowing this was the first step in encouraging human obedience. Plant an idea in their brain and they'll believe it grew there on its own.

****

"It was me," Nettie continued, "that had all three of them nicely fixed up in the empty flat below us. I got Trixie to leave a kitchen window open at the back. Her mother knew all about it but left them to it."

"I know, I know," said Scally, "I know. It's a great story. One of my favourites, especially the part where the fox slaughters every rat in the building. I owe that family a debt of gratitude.

What do you want me to do?"

"Go back down to the flats tonight, get in the way I showed you. and gently, in a very controlled self-disciplined manner, take the last little cub in your mouth and...."

"What!"

"I can't do it, Scall, I simply haven't the strength. What are you shivering about? I thought you said you'd had your jelly."

"I'm still out breath. OK. OK. OK. Hazel's shown me films on YouTube about having some things in your mouth, a dog's mouth that is, not for the purpose of eating it. OK, as I say, it's pay-back time. Hope the thing's not too big. But if you can hold one in your fine pedigree mouth, Nettie, I suppose I can as well. I'm pedigree down one side as well, don't forget, even if I'll never know which one."

"Bravo! Take it to the tree in the woods where we leave their food. That's where I put the other one. But you must go soon, Scall. That bitch will be locked up at night so you'll be safe now but she'll be on my scent in the morning which will lead her to the empty flat below us and the remaining wee cub for sure. And it will help to remember it's not a 'thing.'"

"Understood. Now you get home, Nettie, and leave everything to me. And could you bring another bit of bone out next time, when you're feeling better? They don't get my signals at home about real bone requirement. They just don't. I simply won't touch that squeaky thing. I've tried being subtle about it. Fat lot of good it hasn't done me."

"Human obedience won't happen overnight Scal. Thought transference to humans takes careful preparation, centuries, to begin with, after we first started getting along with them. I'd got Trixie and her mum pretty well tuned in to my needs before we moved here. When I'm better, we'll start on your family; the thoroughly trustworthy Hazel, then her turbulent mum...."

"And her father-in-law's infernal sodding fiddle. I almost can hear it up here. It sounds like cat's guts literally being torn out the whole time, Nettie."

"I wouldn't know. Goodnight, Scallywag the Proud, the Brave, of Quick Brain and Vanishingly Fast Feet…and Acute Hearing…and…anything I've missed out?"

"You forgot the Dribbling, for once."

"I didn't want to suppress it. Not with an upcoming mouthful of small furry mammal to contend with. A profuse flow of saliva will rapidly disperse the scent of master Reynard in your mouth, Scal, making it undetectable by daybreak. These cubs aren't made of old socks, you know."

"I do know. I have as good a nose as you, Nettie. And Hazel tells me everything she knows as well. You seem to have perked up."

"Your jokes are so awful sometimes, Scal, but I'm beginning to feel some get-up-and-go returning to my bad leg. Thank you for that, as well as everything else of course…Good dog, you Skallywag!"

Scally and Nettie Sort Things Out

"The whole point about dog obedience," boomed Colonel Rori McSwiggan, retired, in a voice which Hazel's Mum found increasingly fascinating, "is to give them leadership. The rope, or whatever connects you with a dog's collar; it isn't called a lead for nothing. It teaches their simple minds respect from the word go, from which stems trust and loyalty. Which, with purely physical reprimand kept to a necessary minimum, stimulates obedience. I well remember, boys and girls and your mum's, someone telling me, under fire in Helmand Province Afghanistan…."

Hazel's mind began to wander, the Colonel's voice put her to sleep, or maybe it was his after-shave lotion, tinged with drink, which was very much like the one used by her Dad…and seemed to fill the whole room…and she began to think about her own, her very own Hannibal…outside on his warm cork mat…what had love, sleep-overs and nice bath-times got to do with loyalty, respect and obedience, she wondered dreamily. McSwiggan's red face and white hair reminded her of a poached egg.

"Wasn't he gooood," purred Hazel's mum afterwards, on the way to Ballet at the community centre.

"Christ! What was that?" she suddenly blurted. "Must have been a small dog crossing the road. Nearly ran it over. Did you see it? Shot out in front of me like a blur. Gave me such a fright. Just as well we're nowhere near the house or it could've been Hannibal. He doesn't seem to mind so much nowadays, does he, having to spend punishment time outside the house at night? Are you asleep, Hazel? Wake up we're almost there."

"Mmmmmm. This bone's great, Nettie. Great to have you back. I've missed you. Not just the bones I mean."

"I know what you mean."

"A-ha. As perspicacious as ever. Excuse me. Glad someone ...eshcuse me...can read my mind. Can't read it myself shometimes, too impulsive...excuse me...."

"It's all right, Scally. Gnaw away there and dribble on. Have it all. I'm well fed. They've really looked after me. Mmmm. This is so like old times."

"But it's not. Is it? "

"You're right. There's a new day dawning for us dogs. That 'perspicacious'...that's a new word for you."

"It's one of Hazel's."

"I don't suppose she got it from the Master of Hounds."

"She's started saying it about me. I'm learning to look as if I understand her. Which I always did...But obviously, I neither comprehend nor bark, or even pee in her language. Not that it matters the shlightesht at shleepovers and bath-times. It hashn't mattered shince the day I was first found."

"Precisely. Thought transference at work. Tick done. Top prize. Hannibal. Puddings later. Finish off the bone now, Scally. Aaaaalways reward smart behaviour, however trivial. And, more difficult, aaaalways show approval, personal approval, even if sometimes you have to scold lapses in behaviour like squeeky bones. These don't necessarily indicate a personality lapse. You look as if you're about to doze off, Scall. Am I talking too much? I must be sounding like Hazel's mum. I feel so bonny being back with you again."

"Me too, Nettie and thish T-bone is absholutely shuperb as well...I wash lishtening to you, but transhported out of my shelf at the shame time, that's all. I only looked half ashleep. No offenche."

"None taken."

"I'm learning, slowly, not to take so much offence myself, Nettie, especially when Hazel's mum shoves me outside onto my mat for some shtupid shodding reason. Of course she's no idea about the two of ush shpending half the night together up here at the dump sometimes, shorting things out."

"Waiting patiently for the dawn of human obedience."

"Is that someone I should know?"

"No hurry, Scall. No hurry."

"Hope it's not tomorrow, Netts, I need a day or two off. To get my head round the new bone...and...and all thish new... shtuff...we've been doing."

Plobster Days
and
Plobster Ways

The Soddenish Islands' home grown news,
educational & variety supplement

Habitat 'n' That

Excerpts from a spiked brochure

THE SODDENISH ARCHIPELAGO is set like a clutch of pearls in the west North Sea, a vital node in the maritime portage between the northern isles of Scotland and Iceland. It's abundant fresh water and profusion of the medicinal herb Bersercus Toxcoitus, used for dehiscence (then common is sea-going cattle), ensured a vigorous hybridisation between maritime in-comers and the original Mode 3 homo harris indiginates.

The archipelago comprise one large island, Plobster, and a great number of islets and inlets. The general impression of the Island has been described as "one immense peat bog with notches cut into it to afford shelter for the inhabitants to eke out their spare frames."

The interior from side to side (so-called) is occupied by scraggs and ridges and of Horsemarine and Labradorite. Deer and extinct Auk's beaks abound in the hills. Geese lay each other's eggs.

Strong sea currents course throughout the islands causing regular shipwrecks; from square riggers of a bygone age to today's unvaluable sea-bottom seeking nuclear submarines.

Today, freedom from "hypocrisy, hugger-mugger and peek-a-boo", as well as being outwith the EU's convergent rationing zone, are big attractions. So too are latter day reminders of spiritual wealth in the form of stone age rings, hochs, brochs, frochs, and corbelled burial chambers, stalled and unstalled.

A night of peril, bravely endured and freshly told

"The glass fell abruptly just after we'd finished Bunty's seaweed flan. Looking out of the kitchen window, a huge granite sarcen of a cloud had gathered above the Screes of Dunbumman and was making its way down to Badlipster, Badfilmster, and us.

"An hour later it was blowing a force 12. Whole cabbages were ripped off the dyke. The spire of St Sphagnum's was carried away by a crot of kelp and clouds of wild oats obscured the sun.

"The rivets on the generator flange that adjusted the go-by sheared due to crystalization, jamming the big ends up against the half shaft. The bucket valve that normally prevents this happening was choked with fluff and the explosive build up of steam in the main tubes blew the roof off the cowshed.

"Bunty, myself a the two walrus pup huddled round the one remaining paraffin stove and filled a pail with marbles from the dresser.

"By morning it was spent and so were we. Foot high drifts of spleenthort, banjo and foggy-toddler were strewn over hedge pond and ditch. The repair to the cowshed took so long that the arctic pigeons which usually roost there had to find temporary accommodation in the ruined stanchions of a nearby distillery."

EDITOR'S NOTE: There is an old norse saying: "An Ingeborg hogstader odscoltje Kroken. Fartlek inder bredbyn." Of course this is no truer then than it was today.

ꜰʟᴏᴛꜱᴀᴍ (&) Jᴇᴛꜱᴇᴛ
cultural glimpses

Plobster, twinned with Scheidt-sur-Mere in Belgium, is to hold a modest Arts festival. A special tent is being prepared by chief Sponsor Horsisarsis on his front deck of his yacht Iowna.

Sandra and Amanda will play *Unque Que Paroles Contra la Sostambule* with the Quattuor saxophones de Dingwall. It's intricate weavery, derived from Gnostic gospels, takes us from Palestine to Spain and thence to the Butt of Stockins in our islands. Where we traded our Soddenish herring for their Iberian salt.

Excerpts from the newly re-translated *Bunionaga Sagas of Desparate Half-Dan* have been re-scripted as a pageant play.

Sigurd Clothface encounters a raiding party sent by Noway's King Halfof which includes Hamish Horseleggs, Widewall Kale and Madadsadadperson. St Sphagnum tries to intervene but is carried off by his half brother Rollon-Rollof and roasted alive. Last words:"What kind of fuel am I?"

Home threads, as well as some from abroad, will be featured in a fresh fash splash by Doggi. Try these on for starters. PVC off the shoulder mini-pants with yellow studlettes. Shrill green stilettos sure to blend in and work well in Bog O'Scyrf. Pink puffed chest wigs, full length, with choulched braces, pay homage to Bronzetorso and confirm Doggi's place as modern man's best trend friend.

Good fashion isn't just about gorgeous cut, fiery lapels and bold piping. Sometimes it's more of a kind of half remembered amaphorism, a floating touch, a sparkling mood. Not that we abhor a re-vamp, and I quote: "These clothes are a narrative module combining ascribement, felicity and suction to seduce the gaze and imitate the imagination. (Gulp) Prix de Plobster. "Slack blue tights (Isn't it the other way around? Ed) worn with a cape length choker of fried onions left overnight in pig's gravy (This is mis-placed from the food page, surely. Ed)

Council News
Aspected Training Courses in Transitional Management
Locus: Bloodvista primary school annexe

The Assessment & Control Division are about to action quality management updates to improve the client/provider split.

December
Purchasing requirements for non-purchasing managers
(See under FLAP.)

February
Tailoring financial skills for purchasing non-managers
(See also under GIT)

March

Focused re-distribution of per-assessment guidelines: HUMP

All Previous October

Assessment of pre-validation criteria: CSAR
Coat-hanger size-change app cyberisation module: LIMP
Registration of remaining common-place manual data
(For those hard of hearing)
Non-manual consumerisation handling. (CRAMP)

April

Validation of pre-selected management cohort (BM)
Phased start up of proposed white flag requisitioning camps

ANNALES OSPADALES

News and notes from the Plobster lying-in hospital.
(And gin Dispensary)

An awkward moment in theatre

You could have heard a lawnmower drop in the labour ward as Byong Hak Yu, handsome and popular Japanese locum replacement for Sir Spenciary Ligament scrubbed and gloved up. Bosoms of all sizes, where present, heaved as postman, poet and anaesthatist Lachlan McHachencough put the patient to sleep with his elegy *To a Lost Peatbog*.

No-one had ever attampted a synchronous stenosis of both Amygdala to eliminate non-Hodgkin's Lymphoma in a primigravida. "Give me...something...to hold." Yu muttered implicitly. Sister Eve Frys, though raven haired, statuesque and an experienced nun was a novice at stereo-tactic surgery and hand him a Bunsen burner by mistake which he flung back in her face with a brittle, even brutal gesture. One of the burner's split pins brushed her damask cheek which began to bleed profusely. She was immediately replaced by Sister Ingeborg (of the songs) whose bronze tan and ready sense of fun soon defrosted the tense scene.

During a pause in the procedure, while an episode of gastro-prognosis was being treated with mucous concentrates, Byong surveyed enigmatically the endless humps of broken up turf, dilapidated pet stacks and shell middens that were strewn around the bleak landscape that lay beyond the Dispensary dyke.

"He mused: "How can a break randscape such as this sustain a popuration, rong term, if they all breed like Flys?"

Up Before the Shrieve

fIRST CASE

Patient still unconscious after operating table leg nearly sawn off in error

THE CURIOUS CASE of a bungled miscalculectomy came up before the Shreive last week.

The operation involves a biopsy of the knee. The pod supporting the limb on the operating room table became partially detached during the procedure and started to slide downwards. The surgeon Mr Smuir continued with his work, kneeling with one knee on the floor. The court heard that it was his normal practice, while on secondment in Papua, to suture paddle blade injuries in this way. When it was discovered that Mr Smuir, in addition to the biopsy, had also removed part of the operating table leg, alarm bells were immediately raised.

It turned out that the operating table room leg had been encased in plaster cast before the operation to prevent fatigueability. In the poor lighting conditions at knee level, the cast round the table leg looked so similar to that encasing the patient's knee that a portion of it was included in the surgeon's field of excision. "Exactly why was the operating table leg in a plaster of Paris in the first place?" asked Shrieve Fergus McTaint not unreasonably.

SMUIR	They're very sophisticated pieces of equipment, sir. Fitted with a range of monitors.
McTAINT	Understood. And can you tell the court what happened next?
Smuir	Well as I say, when we were appraised that a notch had been cut out of the table leg, this immediately raised technical concerns and I asked one of the staff nurses to come over and steady it right away.
McTAINT	Steady what?

SMUIR	The leg, sir.
MCTAINT	Whose leg?
SMUIR	The operating table leg, your honour.
MCTAINT	I see, yes. But what had happened to the patient's leg meanwhile?
SMUIR	It was still unconscious, in a manner of speaking, due to the anaesthetic.
MCTAINT	And was this caused or accelerated by the defective table leg?
SMUIR	Only a post-mortem will tell us that, sir.
MCTAINT	But the patient's not dead yet, surely. Was her leg jolted during this mishap?
SMUIR	No. As I say sir, it was the pod holding the patient's leg that was jolted, leading to its partial detachment.
MCTAINT	Not the one that nearly got sawed off then.
SMUIR	No sir. That was the patient's leg. And it's looking perfectly all right now.
MCTAINT	The damage to the pod then, had been sustained previously?
SMUIR	Previous to what your honour?
MCTAINT	Look here. I usually ask the questions in this court. I'll need time to consider this new issue very carefully/ Court adjourned for luncheon.

Second Case

The Gropium shortage case. Dr Smuir's cyclic evidence? Related mishap.

McTAINT   Dr Smuir, where were you on the morning in queeeestion. So sorry, I do apologise.
Must be the pate we had for lunch repeating on me. Careful now.

SMUIR   I parked my Jowett in a lay-by for a smoke, sir.

McTAINT   Why?

SMUIR   Overstress sir. The Thrapple family always leave me exhausted and heart sick. For one thing there's Linda's hernia, then there's Frank's hypovolaemia and Mark's hypothermia....

McTAINT   Doctor, the court understands, there's no need...

SMUIR   ...their mother's refractive dyspraxia not to mention her sister's flagrant dyspepsia. And...

McTAINT   *Oh god my whole lunch feels about to come up.*
DOCTOR

SMUIR   Eppie's whiff, Uncle Lino's chloroma, and Sigmund's gurning melancholia.

McTAINT   *Starting to feel faint. Hot flush. Can't be, Had all the pills first thing this morning.*
DOCTOR DOCTOR
(BUUUURRRP) Sorry...Doctor, the court is only too well aware...

SMUIR   And in the afternnoon I had to perform a Happles craniotomy

McTAINT   Doctor, I really must stop you there.
Where's the hanky?

SMUIR   But that's just it.

McTAINT   What?
Got it

SMUIR	That's why the operation went wrong.
McTAINT	Did it? But I thought....
	Where are we now. Where the hell's the notes?
SMUIR	Having opened the cranium and lifted the flap forward, I severed the hydriform plexus with toothed forceps and was beginning to dissect Hoare's fascia when....
McTAINT	*Whose? Where's that.? Where do horses come into it? Fucking belt's so fucking tight....*
SMUIR	But the tunica elastica was fragmentary and blood began to well out of the wound.
McTAINT	*God no. I hope no photographs exist. My feet are afloat. Must get the court trousers elasticated.*
SMUIR	I called for more Gropium. But there was none.
McTAINT	DOCTOR DOCTOR WILL YOU PLEASE....
SMUIR	Someone my mistake had previously sawn a leg off the filing cabinet and it was in the workshop getting re-welded
McTAINT	NO NO NO NO. I SIMPLY WON'T HEAR ANY MORE SAWN OFF CASES IN THIS COURT. They have gone beyond my jurisdiction. Dr Smuir, you are excused. The court will rise. *Fasten the trousers first. Aaaah soothing Perrier water. Aaaah my hameau in Avignon.*

Third Case

Shrieve McTaint and the plethora of instances

"Why," demanded Shrieve Fergus McTaint of the hapless new depute Fiscal, "do you waste the court's time with this plethora of instances in which, if I'm not mistaken, the accused has little or no *pro bono* connection? *There, young man, get your teeth into that.*

Fiscal depute	I submit with respect sir, that would depend on how the court views the medical evidence.
McTaint	But there hasn't been any. *Has there?*
Fiscal depute	I call upon Dr Campbell McMingen, a forensic pathologist
McTaint	*Oh no. Photos of stiffs now. Not to mention other grisly productions*
Fiscal depute	Are you Dr Campbell McMingen?
McMingen	Yes.
Fiscal depute	And how many post mortems have you done?
McMingen	Thousands.
McTaint	*UUUgh, Don't get him started. Deep breath. New elasticated court trousers working great.* Indeed. And could you summarise the results of your examination please.
McMingen	The body was that of a fit young adult male weighing 6 stone 12 pounds. No external injuries. The brain showed....
McTaint	Wait, isn't that rather light for a fit young adult? *My father weighed that when dying of cancer.*
McMingen	Er...yes...I suppose it is. *Smart man, what could have happened? I did the post mortem two years ago.*

91

McTAINT	Well, how do you account for it?
McMINGEN	Well....
	Got it.
	I must have weighed the body after
	dissection and evisceration.
McTAINT	*EEEEAAARP. Oh no.*
McMINGEN	Retaining some of the vital organs in a bucket....
McTAINT	*UUUURRGF, that bloody pate again. What do they do with it?*
McMINGEN	....for further examination and toxicology.
McTAINT	Pardon, Quite quite quite. If the defence has no objection, we can take the rest of the medical evidence as read, can we not Mr Depute?
FISCAL DEPUTE	If the court so pleases, yes of course.
McTAINT	You can go now Dr McMingen you may stand down, thank you.
	BBBEEEAAARCH. Those thermal tights were a big mistake.
McMINGEN	But I swore to tell the whole truth sir. I feel I must point out other salient features....
McTAINT	Doctor, you are excused. Please go.
McMINGEN	But...
McTAINT	Please step down. The court is adjourned.
	Must make for the lavvy. Damned difficult with all these robes and the wig on. Water water water.

fourth Case

Shreive hacks onto oldest inhabitant

THE FOSSILISED REMAINS of a unique animalicule have been un-covered wile digging out the foundations for a grotesque mew perplexiglass bus stop outside the newsagents. While neither mammalian nor even vertebroid, it nevertheless appears to have a proto-penis, the oldest yet known in these Islands.

"It's definitely not a ventral fin, nor is it for urinating round the corners of the crevices it once inhabited," said Les Twistagen of the Bunns museum of Farther Learning.

There was much excitement locally until the sole centenarian in the archipelago, Angus McSphagnumsen, pointed out that the oldest proven genitalia on the island were in fact his. Unable to be persuaded that the whole thing was a misunderstanding, he instigated a case of slander against the bus stop's owners, the Horsisarsis Foundation, which came up before the Shreive. After a heavy luncheon, of hake and haddock, and with the depute fiscal indisposed, Shreive Fergus McTaint forcefully led out the evidence.

MCTAINT	Is your name Agnus McSphangnumsen?
MCSPHAG	No it is not.
MCTAINT	Kindly answer the question Mr Mc...er Mc Sphagnumsen.
MCSPHAG	It's Angus, your worshship, the first name, not Agnus.
MCTAINT	Of course. I'm sorry Mr McSphagmun....And so forth....I'll begin again. Are you Angus Mc...Mc Sphagmason .. no no SphagMUNsen, I mean?
MCSPHAG	No no its...
MCTAINT	Yes yes. I meant Sphagnumsen all along, Angus McSphagnumsen?

MCSPHAG	Yes thank you.
MCTAINT	Is that the correct pronumciation of your name? *BBUUURP*
MCSPHAG	What?
MCTAINT	Pronunce...prooon-OOUUNCE...excuse me, is that how you call yourself?
MCSPHAG	I do, please.
MCTAINT	Good. So sorry *BEEEAAARP* I do apologise *hatch...hatch....hatch* I think *aaasch aaascha HATCHOO* Slight cough this morning. Bit of fish caaaaught *HATCHOO AT...CHACKA* in the throat. Mr McSphag...hag..the court will take a short adj... *CHOUARN HOCH HACH A-TISHU* adjournment. *HACHA HATCHA HATCHCA RAAFA ACGHA....* **Ftoon**.

Fishbone lodged in veteran's cheek. Shrieve McTaint is now in traction with a direct inguinal hernia. Prosecution suspended.

fifth Case

Up before the Shrieve last week was the case of an interior decorator whose nose got trapped in a sash cord causing a lacerated nostril for which he claimed damages. The defence pleaded that a diagnosis of pico-noseola was a pre-disposing factor, hastening the onset of an otherwise occult nostrilar keratosis-in-situ that was the true cause of the nasal lesion.

Shrieve Fergus McTaint asked Dr Smuir for clarification of the sub-divisions likely to be met with.

McTaint	Dr Smuir, we have heard from Professor Polyp that, from a nosological viewpoint. a nostril, as we know it, or perhaps I should refer to it as them, in the every day parlance, may, at times, be considered not to be a nostril at all as such; but rather, for the purposes of disease class-ification, one of not a few otological sub-categories. What is your experience of this?
Smuir	I don't know what he's talking about, your honour. To me, a nostril, or both of them, preferably as you suggest, are crucial to nasal function. Without them, what have you? Neither sub-categorisation nor a sense of burnt toast. This is not a chicken and egg situation in my view.
McTaint	But could it not, as the defence insists, be nosologically the other way round?
Smuir	The other way round what?
McTaint	Giving primacy to the part rather than the parcel, if you see what I mean.
Smuir	Can't say that I do.
McTaint	Let me put it this way. Is a symptomless pre-

condition, nosologically to be categorised as being equivalent to, say, being born with one leg, which is also, in a manner of speaking, asymptomatic? If so, then neither condition is, as such, a nosological entity or even a disease process wouldn't you say? And therefore not subject to civil litigation in this court.

SMUIR   Unless you pick your nose too much and your keratosis-in-situ becomes invasive. Or you fall downstairs.

McTAINT   So pico-noseola doesn't come into it noso-logically in this particular case unless you actually have the habit or have a pre-disposing congenital keratotic condition?

SMUIR   More or less.

McTAINT   Or you leave your prosthesis, say, in a taxi.

SMUIR   But that's hardly a syndrome.

McTAINT   Even in the presence of clinical melancholia?

SMUIR   In my opinion, a degree of melancholia is normal from time to time and not to be medicalised for profit.

McTAINT   Even if it becomes syndromatic by association with other more acceptably profitable pre-conditions, as heretofore?

SMUIR   But that's an entirely hypothetical situation, is it not, with regard to the evidence put before me this morning?

McTAINT: That will be for the court to decide, Dr Smuir. No further questions. That's quite enough for now. The court will rise for luncheon.

THE
BUNIONAGA SAGAS

Desperate Halfdan's fall from Grace

Re-translated for every day usage
by Magnus McSlangmunsen

THE EARLIEST KNOWN versions of the Bunionaga Sagas were inscribed on rods of sea-food vellum in the tenth century by frenzied clerics at Bunionvoe. (Present day Plobster, in the Soddennish Islands.)

This is multi-pronged narrative, taking in many different elements of life on these islands at that time; when yamma-yamma and derring-do, not to mention ramping and pillage, were as pervasive round here as of now.

And, as many have said before and since, "Faint heart never won fat lady."

But poor Sigurd Clothface, son of Widewall Kale, was faint-hearted. Fainthearted to a fault, and melancholic to boot. He was the only nobleman who never managed to live up to his rank and title: Earl of Bigsister. Unable to see any point in the slicings and hackings continually going on, he did what he could to bring about a change of social consciousness. To this end, he availed himself of a Sauceress, his toxic aunt Swoona, who had foretold, from the remains of a dog's breakfast, that the whole of Rollon-Rollof's realm in the Soddennish islands (as they were not yet so-called) was soon to be engulfed by semi-precious men from Northern Suitland in the south. Who lived in weal-Boroughs.

Sigurd, moved by his Aunt's divination, became an anti-hero and administered bad forecasts, mainly by the oral route, but also in the form of nerd pamphlets and agit-prop (as it was not yet so-named).

Being toxic as well as illiterate, aunt Swoona enlisted the aid of the beautiful Bunionaga, previously cook to King Halfof, in the hope of assembling from Sigurd's febrile handouts, something to be used as propaganda for the Earls around her; currently clamouring and plundering to determine their own self determination without recourse to any of these new-fangled, newly suited, southern weal Boroughs.

Finally, confronted by an oracular fork in the road, Sigurd Clothface became a transvestite nun and called himself Desperate Halfdan to avoid his kinsmens' ridicule, But unbridled sarcasm reliably goaded him into action and Bunionaga found it hard to keep up with demand for popular verses and stories about Halfdan's anti-Suititic prejudice and his later infatuation with Frosenfude.

Ross Ossage (Bog o' Bigbag Herald) writes in a clear manner, *"Magnus MacSlangmunsen's novel translation is intended for every day hyper-market carparks and the modern laundromat. Its die-verse forms echo both the pagan splendour as well as the knife edge immediacy of the original. In Bunionaga's sagas of Desperate Halfdan, we glimpse, as through a peep-hole, a people on the cusp of a vertiginous point in time."*

WHO'S HO IN BUNIONVOE

ARS COONCIL	After the death by inanition of Snorri Sponsor person, hordes of ailing poets & playwrights kept alive in his Halls on a diet only of silver
BUNTY THONGLIP	Notedly over-strident Bunioniste songstress
BOGNOSE SICK-TOOTH	Offers son's niece to Olaf Tit-Bit
CATMEAT SNORKEL	Eccentric underwater vegan raider
EARL DOGFIN	Bane of Halfdan's life, for piercing sarcasm
EGON BACONSEN	Split roasted in his own fish shop
ERIC STRAYBALLS	This wretch's treachery led to death of Earl Thikkokk.
FETYD CAFF	One of two divergent twins. They set up inns on Cruiseader route to Bunionusalem
FROSENFUDE OF THE SONGS	Egon Baconsen's widow. Mother of Desperate Halfdan's seven dwarfs Died in wool, suffocated by sheep's fluff

HORS FEDDOGS	Seal hunter. Dogs died breaking wind
KING HALFOF	Legendary Lord off all Bunion; Slaughtered St Sphagnum, cooked & ate him
LOTTE CARFERRIES	Beloved of Rollon-Rollof
NJOTALOTTE CARFERRIES	Jilted mistress of Rollon-Rollof
ROLLON-ROLLOF	Roaster & old sea dog. Burnt six others' wives. Futile marriage to Fishnet Stokkin
SKYDD TOE-HOOK	Waif and one time wife of sage Fridjoff Splitrouserson.
TEN-ESSAY ERNIEFJORD	Dark skinned poet, pedant and cobbler Owed his sole to the Company Store First Norse crooner to wear a bow tie
URS YULAKJIT	Halfdan's bastard child of a Nospyk Eskimo

HOW IT ALL BEGAN FOR DESPERATE HALFDAN

THE SAGE beneath the stunted oak said,
"Jings, now here's a good y'un:
I'll tell of a man with seven long ships
Who couldn't lick the skin off a rice pudden."

The heavens laughed when he was born, under the kitchen table.
Tough decision, a blunt incision and the mid wife-won at Scrabble.

His father sang, from dusk till dawn, folk songs by Bobdylan.
But folks upstairs preferred Joan Baez & adopted Vietnamese chillan.

3 times round he went the poles; thrice 3 times thrice times 3.
And each time out he came back in with a rhyming dictionary.

For his aunt, a Lallans poetease, "Upstairs," his bourne was bidden.
"Or the rag tag bairn o' a keltie's pouk'll get his heid
                    first doon the midden."

And sae at schule he kent his merks. His snotters were of iron
Hengin' doon frae a neb lik a prune, grafeety defy'in.

His quarrel with Earl Dogfin

In fulsome May Dogfin rode by, the azure skies unclouded
On a fretful horse fresh from intercourse
And this is what he shouted.
"What ho, aloof, art nun or poof?" he laughed and snapped his
fan. "I'll have his yetts for garters yet," sighed Desperate Halfdan.

There was Snorri asleep with Nose-Rope, living together in sin.
When all of an April evening, Halfdan came stumbling in
Carrying a blood red cheese cake, the head of Earl Dogfin.

"I've crimsoned him, the bastard," he declaimed with a frown.
"He'll ne'er call me a transvestite again,
In his Fair Isle dressing gown." That's how
Halfdan the Desperate did chop unbridled sarcasm down.

Desperate Halfdan at the Edinburgh Festival

And so we descended from Mousevista and parked by a bay of cars.
Before ripping open a supermarket, holding up high in our hands
the booty. Then it was Egon Baconsen's chip shop; gorging on their
sisters' spiked blood puddings. Nothing between us, 'specially the
one with the searingly dark black hair.
Love those Iberian lasses.
Those black tresses, raven as well as riven.
Pity Aeonghas the Hebridean couldn't have come. He'd have loved it.
Lapped it up.
Always going on about booty of one sort or another, he was,
As well blondes with their golden helmets.
Ah those golden helmets. Metallic but listless.
My mother once knitted him one on her deathbed.and had it
quilted. But never got a word of thanks. Not even a mention,
anywhere in his peoms.
Of which there were plenty. You'd have thought he might.

Bunionvoe Nuns' Sea Raid

The otter bitch sniffed the meadow
The sea cow looked forlorn
And the stars shone down on Skyd Toe-Hook
The fake Deaconess of Mourne.
And the Sauceress Bunty Thong-lip, brewing up a storm.

"For weeks we ploughed through mist and filth
Our eagle spars set for Grimsby.
And how our hearts soar like a beach-Elk mare
During a week's keen rutting in the forests of Trollbergen."

Ross Ossage writes, *"There is some discontinuity between these two fragments and many would consider the second stanza, as well as some others to follow, to have been inserted at a later date by a different writer. Elk mares rutting (but not rhyming) in the woods are OK. Nuns rutting in Grimsby are not OK, even if it's only for a week."*

Miraculous Burial of Pagan Saint

There's some old, ruined fish nets to the South of Toothaigh Mor
By Voe of Plughole, Cnoc and Scroo and Filla.
Where the moon frowns down in a whore frost gown,
But your shlang's like a frozen pillar.

Beneath the nets lie St Sphagnum,
Of sacred memory
Roasted alive with Horseleggs,
Outside, at Minusthree.

From Flotta to Foulis Filmster,
From Frail to Fucksakesnoe,
Sweet Bunionaga, in sealskin Jaeggar,
Hid in the longship's prow.

With an urn and the ash, an axe
and some cash, she made her silent vow.

To make a monument, deep in sand
Supported by loose timber.
Covered with nets in memoriam
For a fisherman we'll all fondly remember
For his love of the hints of autumn tints
As the nights drew in, in early late September

Ross Ossage writes, *"The last stanza is almost certainly another of those preposterous insertions made at a much later date. This style of naturalistic bilge became known as 'Bunion-Ingrid' after a short lived prudish abbess of that name who tried to clean up these sagas. St Sphagnum also fell for Frosenfude in a big way and when she repudiated his more pagan proposals, (such as dressing up for the night in fish net tights), he tried to carve up the seven dwarfs she'd had with Halfdan and the whole family flew into exile at Danish Tarzanahagen.*

HALFDAN AND THE NUNS' TRIP TO DUNFAMINELIN FOR THE SPRING SALES

AUNT SWOONY took the tiller, Turkey Stoffin trimmed the sails.
And Desperate Halfdan spat on the tide.
A long boat full of plunder, half off blouses, zips asunder.
"At last," he felt, "I've joined a winning side."

They'd murdered the dressmakers, Starbucks, the undertakers
His melancholy definitely shifting. With a shout that
shocked the gannets, he surveyed the jeans and Janets
And wondered whose mock surplus he'd soon be lifting.

"Perhaps"... "There's nae perhaps, or I'll navel oot yer chapps,"
His inner Lallans Daemon found him sayin'.
"Git doon there, git oan under, stuff the loot 'n' stuff
the plunder, A sonsie wife wud cure ye o' a' that slayin'."

Ross Ossage writes, *"Readers following the plot so far and therefore on full alert for spurious insertions of "Bunion-Ingrid", will doubtless have glutted themselves to the full on verse three. But this metrical buffoonery nevertheless accurately foretells Halfdan's later long term relationship with the legendary Frosenfude, resulting in their seven dwarfs.*

Desperate Halfdan and Splitparts Glumperson reconciled

One day, Desperate Halfdan had a word with Splitparts Glumperson. He needed help with a summer trip to central Suitland in order to take revenge on the clans for the hewing of his niece's legs off. (Anna Horseleggs)

"Not sure I'm up to it," muttered Glumperson, whittling away at a knotty oak stump, "too many prayer stools to turn out for the new religions. But tell you what, I'll let you have those six Moron cut-throats I got in Norbonne last year...provided...."

"Provided what?" Halfdan smelt a rat & drew his pencil & paper.

"Provided you find a worthy husband for my sister, Frosenfude"

"I thought there might be some problem, Splitparts. But I also thought she was grudgingly married to Egon Baconson."

"Sliced to strips only last week. Served up in his own chip shop. Burned to a cinder. By your kinsmen."

"In that case I'll have her for myself. Always fancied her ravenous dark looks and her ample soft collection of whale-pin brooches."

Ross Ossage writes: *"Here again, with the whale-pin brooches nonsense, we have a choice example of Ingrid the short lived abbess cleaning up Bunionaga."*

The next piece is written as dialogue, to be declaimed by two raving poets at feasts, etc. With the addition of a third person (in large print) to shout out the action and scenery, etc.

Bunionaga, (or more likely Bunion/Ingrid) can justifiably claim, in the next maudlin extract, to have penned a precursor to the entire realm of post-modern psycho sit-com. This almost filmic fragment depicts Halfdan and Frosenfude's fraught voyage into exile, in an open boat (with their seven infant dwarfs) to escape St Sphagnum's unwelcome fixations.

FROSENFUDE QUESTIONS HALFDAN'S PLANS

NIGHT, DEEP FOG, OARS SPLASHING

FROSENFUDE	If only we'd navigated northwards, we'd have got some wind off-shore.
	THEY EMBRACE
	I just don't feel like it at the moment.
HALFDAN	It won't take but a minute. Oh all right then. Here, hold these.
	HE TAKES A HAMMOCK OFF A HOOK ON THE RIGGING HOLDING THE 7 INFANT DWARFS
FROSENFUDE	But they've all been sick on me twice tonight already. You feed them for a change. I'll trim the spars.
HALFDAN	With what?
FROSENFUDE	What do you mean what?
HALFDAN	Trim them...with what?
FROSENFUDE	No, I mean raise them up a bit to catch the slightest breeze. Now you get their feeds ready.
HALFDAN	Look, we simply can't go on feeding all 7 of them. There's scarcely enough fish for the men doing all the rowing as it is. You must understand.
FROSENFUDE	But you never told me about this before. We didn't talk, you should've explained.

106

LATER THAT NIGHT

HALFDAN   That's them all down. The oarsmen sung them
             to sleep. You look like your mother in the frozen
             moonlight.

FROSENFUDE   Don't be so daft. We're in thick fog. There's no
             moonlight at all.

HALFDAN   It's the words of the song, Frosenfude. Get a life.

FROSENFUDE   Are we safe?

HALFDAN   Until daylight unless the wind gets up

THIRD ACTOR WHISTLES, IMITATING A SOFT BREEZE

FROSENFUDE   Thank god for that. Any fish left?

HALFDAN   More than enough as it happens. Like the stars in
             your eyes.

FROSENFUDE   Bloody oarsmen. Can't you get them to shut up?

HALFDAN   That was me.

FROSENFUDE   Sorry. Not the typical repartee of a transvestite nun.

HALFDAN   The transvestiture was a sham in order to receive
             Holy Orders.

FROSENFUDE   Orders to do what?

HALFDAN   To achieve grace.

FROSENFUDE   But you told me earlier she'd died in a fire with all
             the horses.

HALFDAN   Exactly, so I became a nun to abide with her in spirit.

FROSENFUDE   Unbridled sarcasm, then, had nothing to do with it.

HALFDAN   Nothing whatsoever at the time. That came after.

FROSENFUDE   That's all right then. But what on earth had you been
             reading lately? It smacks of St Sphagnum's Gospel
             to me, without the malarkey.

LIGHTNING STRIKES AND A CLAP OF THUNDER.
OARSMEN SHRIEK WITH FRIGHT.
A STORM TEARS THROUGH THE RIGGING.

FROSENFUDE   I'll kill him, I'll kill him, I'll kill him. Kith and kin.

HALFDAN   Why bother. We'll be safe enough now in the East with this following wind. When we get to Tarzanahagen, we can co-found a new dynasty.

FROSENFUDE   We've 7 dwarfs already. I'm getting soaked. Where's the oilskins?

HALFDAN   There's goldmines in Tarzanahagen. The dwarfs will come in handy.

FROSENFUDE   After they've been trained for the priesthood of course.

HALFDAN   Naturally. We could say the oldest was found in a laundry basket by a river in Mesopotamia. Ever been there?

FROSENFUDE   Never even heard of it.

THE LONGBOAT IS SHATTERED BY A FREAK WAVE

CONCLUSION

DESPERATE HALFDAN survived the wreckage of his entire family and crew but ended up insane due to a premature menapostle he picked up while on a pilgrimage to the fabled oiled caves of Kurdo-Iranarab. These grottoes were also held sacred to the Gods of Suitland due to an epic poem dictated (in fits and starts) by Sigmund Einstein, in the primary pre-Data period.

Halfdan lost his shirt when the price of ships went down during the night of the long Suits.

Dogfin's twins overcame their squint. Each married into a good family in Bog O' Bag. They too ended up in suits, but with only one wooden leg between them, they didn't get far. Their progeny colonised Frife, becoming seasonal plouk pickers in the straths.

One day, the now aged Earl of Bunionvoe beseeched one of his granddaughters to pay him a visit at the now ruined Hall at Rubha Gristle. The girl had never left the Borough she had been born in and didn't want to go at all. In a trance, she made this verse:

THE LAST TUNE

"I DON'T WANT to go to Bunionvoe,
I'd rather stay home in Kirkcaldy."

When she inherited the Earldom, it had vanished. She became the sole owner of the last boot shop in Bunionvoe, which by then had re-branded as "Bunionavista" and twinned with Bunionusalem, somewhere in the Levant.

The Adventures of Dr. Strukahrov

The Emigrant Physician

UNDER THE COVER OPERATIONS, SUSPENSE, RAW NERVE AND BARE FLESH,
SOME OF IT STILL ALIVE, ARE BRAIZED INTO THIS FOUR PART MEDICALISED
ROMANCE, PACKED WITH FOREIGN & LOCAL INTRIGUE.

1. **WHO NEEDS A BIG ONE?** This drug-soaked yarn bristles with truely hapless love and bad food. Starting in a vegetarian bistro in Edinburgh's vibrant New Town and casting a trail of human remains, the story heedlessly heads across France to its scorching climax in a Nice crematorium.

2. **DEATH IN GLENROTHES.** Webbed by spewed-up lap-top data, this gobsmacking, cyber-nautic, anatomic/romantic episode will keep you glued to your cushy seats all the way from the freshly painted spars of the Forth Rail Bridge to a tragi-comic denouement in a curtained front room in Glenrothes.

3. **SISTER TROTSKAYA'S APPENDIX.** The emigrant doctor Strukahrov, on the move again, renews by chance a hazardous relationship with an operating room nurse allegedly descended from a Bolshevic military genius. Set in ruined bedrooms and plush safe houses, the action unravels across West Asia, including central Scotland, ending on the Indian sub-continent where the lovers bring the mend home.

4. **RED PHONES AT THE READY.** While an unbelievable secret blood-line drama develops in the diplomatic bags of HQ's High Office, Dr Strukahrov and Sister Trotskaya, neither of them any longer young, step firmly into their next lives in two opposite directions. Not knowing that their separate paths will lead them both to the same place.

fEATURING

EMIL STRUKAHROV	Emigrant physician. 10,002 autopsies, the last two during this mini-novella
MARINA	Long haired adventuress & haven for yachts
SERENA	Matrix of disguise. Voice behind yesterday's newspaper
BRANISLAV	Notorious oligarchic criminal
GIROCEC	Bisexual hardware expert
HINNIE MCHUBRIS	Bootless assassin
SISTER TROTSKAYA	Retired theatre nurse (operations). Allegedly descended from the secret love child of a Bolshevic military genius
HIS EXCELLENCY	Well connected rug dealer and diplomatic blather. Aspiring pulp novelist
IRINA	Shrewd 1st Secretary / aspiring pulp co-author

PART 1

LET US SPRAY

DR EMIL STRUKAHROV, the emigrant physician, carefully put his new passport, visa and work permit into his wallet and set about the incineration and disposal of their previous owner. Rather well traveled, he settled on rural France; the food was so tres good there. And was soon stuffing the frame tubes and handlebars of his folding Dahon bicycle with little cylindrical poly bags of ash and less well carbonised human gunge wrapped round with baco-foil. He bought a TGV ticket to Nice and, the next day, with a few hours to spare before his train to London, called in at a local vegetarian restaurant for breakfast; hoping he might clap eyes on Marina, which he did, looking like a nun in civvies as usual. He bit idly into his bitter scone.

112

Meanwhile, the corpse in the men's lavvy No. 2, below the stairs, was still warm. The cleaner had been wanting to do out the cubicle for the best part of half an hour, he said, after having being cautioned.

"I thought he might be unwell or something and kicked the door, as if by accident, to see what reaction there might be from the other side, but there was none. Just then that foreigner came in and straightaway took up in No. 1, and so I left and went looking for Archie, my boss."

Two of Emil's guiding principles were these: first, Never Trust a Fart (Billy Connolly) and second, Always Close Doors Once You Have Passed Through Them (his own, or so he thought, but so, too, had his father). Life's an On-going No-Turning-back Situation, he continued, dreamingly noting how Marina's long straight hair framed her face as if it were a habit and, good grief, she was even gleaming, in an annunciated sort of a way, at this very precise moment. Think I'll nip into the bog, then try chatting her up.

Well, he thought, as he sat down in the toilet, the smell in here's perfectly awful, what the fucksakes that cleaner do for a living? Then he saw, just on his side of the partition between the cubicles, which didn't quite reach the floor, a small cylindrical white plastic thingy the size of a tube of lipstick.

He leaned forward to pick it up; it turned out to be a nasal spray. He then saw, on the other side of the partition, a hand, palm down on the floor, fingers clenched, the wrist bent back as if bearing weight. Long dark tufts of hair sprouting from the backs of its fingers.

Then, also from the same cubicle, there came a gigantic crapulent bowel sound, immediately followed by the sharp crack and heavy slumping of someone falling forwards and whacking their head on the lavvy door. With the result that the hand that he'd first seen on the other side of the partition, with its closed fist, was now thrust right under the partition onto his side, rotating and opening out as it did so to reveal a good sized lump of hashish, a substance with which Dr Emil Strukahrov was not unfamiliar.

Nor was he unfamiliar, from previous employment, with the sound of persons dropping down dead on the floor. Not being one to Look a Gift Horse in the Mouth, he trousered this unexpected treasure trove without hesitation, it would do nicely for his holiday, and made his way back up the stairs to chat up that woman before the smell became intolerable. His dad had never actually explained to him what a Gift Horse really was, but he knew he'd just encountered one.

In the restaurant upstairs, Marina had her mobile out and was thumbing it like a familiar prick.

"He should be dead by now."

"How long since you gave him the drug?" said Serena, sitting on a park bench miles away behind yesterday's paper.

"About twenty minutes, half an hour."

"Anyone else in there?"

"No. it's a quiet cold morning. The cleaner's been in an out a few times as usual. Otherwise just one other, one of the regulars...he went in a minute or so ago...that's him coming out now."

She tilted the front of the phone in Emil's direction as he came back up the stairs.

"Excuse me, is this yours?" Emil said, indicating a newspaper neatly folded on a chair beside her.

"No you can have it."

"Thanks." He smiled as best he could, though it looked like he was trying to suppress wind, and went to the coffee queue.

"D'you know him?" asked Serena.

"Not well enough to ask him if he'd seen anything unusual in the toilet, no. Now here's something. The cleaner's talking to the boss and they've gone down to the toilets together. Should I hang on?"

"You've got the money?"

114

"Yes."

"Right. Just keep an eye on that bloke then, for a bit. Can you hack his mobile?"

"Probably."

"He might well have heard or otherwise sensed something was amiss if our man was already dead or dying by the time he got in there. He might want to talk about it to someone."

"Do they have fits and thrash about when they die?"

"Not as a rule. But anyone can shit themselves when the white chariot swings low."

"I didn't know you were so spiritual."

There was a pause..."Marina?"

But Marina was speechless. She'd been watching the doctor, in the queue for coffee, reach into his pocket for money and come out with a white nasal spray in his hand as well as loose change. He'd clean forgotten that he'd uplifted this item just before the gift-bearing fist had been thrust into his cubicle and now clumsily tried to replace the spray in his pocket. With visionary clarity, Marina saw his comic fumbling as he succeeded in dropping both spray and coins onto the floor. It was on her mobile too, as she'd inadvertently left it on when she put it down on the table. Quickly she was at his side helping him out while at the same time assessing her chance of relieving him of the spray, without him being aware of it.

The reason being that half an hour ago, in a taxi, it was she who had given this spray to the man now dead in the toilet as part of a deal, saying it was a new way of taking meth-coke. Instead, it had delivered a fatal dose of Paradrenalin-B to his lungs. As she knew it would.

"Here, can I help?"

"Oh, thanks. What a clot I am. Muddle fingers!"

Couldn't have worked out better, he thought as he somewhat absent-mindedly re-pocketed the lethal spray stick and stole a glance down the neck of her blouse.

She jostled him about a bit, accidentally on purpose, to

distract him while picking his pocket. But the stick had gone through a hole in the lining and was unobtainable. Typical cheap jacket, though it looked new.

"Was there anything good in the paper?" she chirped.

> *Maybe he'll take his jacket off at some point. He's got rather a lot on.*

"Nothing. I specially wanted to see the weather."

"You look as if you might be off somewhere. Or have you just arrived?"

"No, on my way...short trip abroad, with the bike."

"So this coffee's your last score before take-off then."

> *Sheer up-frontery often got surprising results.*

"More or less."

> *Not this time.*

But an uneasy sort of furtive grin spread across his face, which, she was later to discover, could just as well have been due to sexual arousal rather than any tribulation he may have felt about nicking a dead man's stash. Guilt was not a condition for which Dr Strukahrov paid house calls.

> *This is a truly beautiful woman, and she seems to be taking an interest in me. Why not try to date her up when I get back?*

"Is the toddler I at times see you with in here...a relation?"

> *Interest in Women's Children Never Fails.*
> *(Another of his dad's Major Maxims.)*

"Yes, she's my sister's. What type of bike is it you've got?"

> *Ditto, with men, according the Special Forces Manuals the world over. Interest to their equipment reliably excites interest and admiration.*

"It's a folder. They're dead easy to take with you on trains."

"So I've heard, especially on TGVs. No fuss if it's all in its wee baggie."

This was another shot in the dark, but she'd noted a small wad of Euros amongst his loose change so it was worth a try.

But again he gave nothing away. She straightened up, pulled down the hem of her homely cardigan, neatly outlining its underlying content, and changed the subject. Noting that his eyeball pupil reaction was both bizarre and inconclusive. The left one dilated all right, while the right seemed stuck at pinpoint. He's in trouble clearly, she thought.

"I blame the weather," muttered Emil, with a stiff upper lip.

"What for?"

"Too cold and wet for a big score. Sticky wicket."

Cricket jokes clearly a wash-out. Usually are with women....

She huddled like a child; it sometimes excites them.

"I'm going to have a refill, can I get you one, or are you in a hurry to go?"

"I think I should ge going, thanks all the same. Train at 12.30. But can I take you up on that the next time we meet? I've seen you here a few times before, have we not?"

His English usage needs a bit of a re-fit....

"We have...good heavens there's two policemen going into the toilet with Archie...he owns the place...whatever do you think's going on? A case for Sherlock, or just routine?"

"I bet they're from the health and hygiene inspectorate, or whatever it's called here. Nothing more. The porridge locally is pure filth, wouldn't you agree?"

Yet, again, as cool as a cucumber.
With nice hair going curly at the sides.

"Where do you usually get your oats? Are you an expert on the subject?"

No sign of having got the joke at all. Can't be British.
Pupils almost back to normal though...almost.

"No I'm just an ordinary doctor...Swedish." In fact Dr Strukahrov was Russian, but it said Sweden on his new passport.

"A specialist in porridge-storage diseases, perhaps?"

This woman seems unusually widely read.

117

"Wish I was. I could afford to offer you dinner and a concert ticket. Instead it will have to be a de-caff re-fill, a brown scone and a walk to the bus stop. Can we save it till I get back?"

"Certainly. I wouldn't dream of doing all that on my own."

"Think I'll push off then, for now. Looking forward to the next time." He hauled off with his folding bike, neatly folded.

Marina thumbed her phone.

"Think I'll tag him. At a distance."

"Why? Is it because he's a Swede by any chance. You're are awful with men. Even when, or is it specially because, you've just murdered one?"

"How do you know he's Swedish?"

"You left your mobile on, silly. I'd let the spray stick go. It would've been discovered in the lavvy anyway. And most people manage to empty them, being so desperate for their hit. So there's little or no danger from it."

"Why did that guy have to be killed?"

"To show that vile bastard Branislav...et al...what and where the limits are; the boundaries within which we all co-operate and move our money about freely up here. To show that we've noticed an acquisitive tendency...poaching on our ground...and trying us out...and that we hope this will dissuade him from any further escapades. As a matter of fact, it was Branislav's kid brother who we bumped off, who he never liked, so he won't be missed in the Organisation. But he was Family, and that's where we'll have hit him, right in the nuts. God, I'll nail him and his henchmens' fucking cocks to the table if they continue sniffing round up here."

"But you could be right", Serena went on, "the very fact your Swede seems to have got hold of the spray, however he did it, does suggest he might be linked to them in some a way or other. Yes...in the circumstances, you may as well see where he goes and who he meets up with. It could reveal more about their Organisation up here. Give us an in. On no account approach him directly though, or you'll be spotted. Keep it clean, petal, unless otherwise instructed."

They signed off and, as she did so, Marina noted her menu button light up briefly, twice. Indicating that some smart-Alec had taken a shot at the firewall. Twenty thumbs later and she'd got the name and pin number for future reference. And in as many minutes, she'd boarded the 12.30 to London at the rear end, having seen, by the tag she'd fixed to his jacket, that Emil was seated at the front.

JUST A LITTLE PRICK

THIS WOULD BE an excellent place for the burial, thought Emil, viewing the vast flat lands around the river Marne at St Marie des Taudres, and at the same time trying to figure out how to improve his chances with that woman in the bistro with whom he now was totally obsessed.

On impulse, slightly stoned, he got out at the next stop, scarcely getting his bike (in its bag) disentangled from the luggage rack in time and only just remembering, at the hotel counter, to try out his new personna in French. He emptied his bike of its manky contents, surrounding them with more layers of baco-foil, had a sandwich, put the remains in his ruc-sac (along with a handy folding shovel) and set off down a little lane off the main road. This ended in an orderly-looking glade of poplars, from which muddy allotments led down to a canal covered with scum.

Perfect, he thought, it's just getting dark, when a thin beam of very bright, excruciatingly bright light, suddenly shone in his face and a male voice, from some distance away, said, "Don't move, don't move an inch; or in your case, you little metric Viking rascal, don't move one centimetre," and he heard two raincoats laughing.

A third raincoat had Emil's ruc-sac off his back and was rustling around inside it, peeling off bits of the foil.

"What's in this....fuuuucking hell....what's this? Uugh. See what he's got in here? What the fuck is this muck, food?"

The raincoats gathered round. The light kept its head.

"Just put all that aside carefully, whatever it is, don't leave any behind, and find that fucking spray stick. That's what we want. Is it there, got it? Good."

He turned to Emil.

"Now, Swede, how did you get this, that's what I want to know. And don't you dare fucking move or you're dead. Go on, tell us, save us time, save yourself a lot of pain. Kick him, some-one."

"I only nicked it honest. It rolled under the partition of a toilet I was in, in Scotland. I never saw the man who had it, no idea who he was. I heard someone falling down in the next door toilet and it just rolled under the partition. Honest, that's it. Who...who are you?"

"Never you fucking mind. Where did you give it him?"

"Give it him? He give it to me more like. It sounded like he'd crapped himself then died and keeled over. Honest."

"But how did he get the spray in the first place? That's what we want to know. Come on, those gals gave it him, didn't they? Then you were assigned to get it back, to prevent the police from getting their hands on your new toy, your latest killer drug."

"Toys? Killer drugs? Look, you're all mixed up, whoever you are. I promise I've no idea what you're on about. A dead hand came under the partition and I took what was in it. That nasal spray and a bit of hash. What's this all about? You want some?" Emil put a hand in his pocket.

"Don't move. OK, I'll believe you. Now you listen. My dear mother's got some nice food, and she said, if you turned out all right, which you clearly have, that you could come round with the gang and share our meal. But she's fussy about body odour, my mother, and hates her guests to have bad breath. So open wide, hold him someone, and lets just freshen you up, if you don't mind, with what's left of this. Open wide and take a deep breath, you lying Scandinavian cunt. How's this for dead hand?"

There was muffled gunfire and the lights went out, one by one, as Marina, who had been following Emil since he'd got off the train at a discrete distance, shot all three raincoats and once more hurried to his side. He was flat out, gasping for breath, just conscious; conscious of his heart beating inside his brain like a bell.

She rolled him on his back, pulled his shirt sleeve up, and swiftly wrapped a velcro tourniquet round his upper arm. Serena was right, not much was left in that spray after its first user had finished with it, because Emil was still alive. She took the vial of Paradrenalin antidote from her body belt, drew the contents up into a syringe, then probed his arm gently for a vein that wasn't yet collapsed.

Emil felt her touch and opened his eyes. Seeing this, she whispered "It's me, from Archie's restaurant. You've been poisoned with that spray. Not enough to kill you. I have the antidote ready. It's intra-venous, I'm afraid. Try and relax your arm. Trust me. Just a little prick."

"Who needs a big one?" he asked in fluent French, but passed out before she could reply. In a half a minute, his pulse, blood pressure, and both pupils stabilised, and he came round. They left the ruc-sac and shovel, with the remains of the Swede Emil had brought with him on holiday, half buried beside the dead raincoats. The police would have fun sorting that one out.

KINKS IN THE CHINKS

BRANISLAV ENJOYED champagne at any time of the day or night, especially on the balcony of his villa overlooking the old part of Nice. But he could take it or leave it, and when he left it, he never bothered re-corking the bottle. Not that there was any likelihood of this after lunch with Girocec, his bisexual hardware handyman.

"Amateurs," Branislav began, "this unnecessary toxicology; spoonfuls of this, nano-quantities of that. What are they trying to show ? How clever they are? When was it ever necessary to kill people with tainted cocoa, strobe lights or sophisticated snorts?"

"Give me the four Bs any day. Bullets, blades, buggery and blunt injury. The traditional skills are almost dying out on us." Girocec's father had also been an assassin.

"Putin hasn't forgotten them, the devil bless him."

"He could have been a Cossack, like me."

"You look more like a Corsican, Giro."

"No, I don't. You're so rude."

"Giro, I've got something for you."

Up on a plasma screen came a sequence of stills and short clips hacked off Marina's previous mobile.

"Here's two of their people heading our way. They evaded our first punch but in the process given themselves away...especially what she's up to...and now we have them firmly in our sights.

"That's Marina, and, unknown to her, she's about to sacrifice that poor bastard there, a Russian doctor under an assumed name, having shagged him almost night and day this past week to break his cover. But there is no cover. He's just a lesser criminal, out of his depth, who got mixed up with her by chance; having picked up in the toilet, God knows how, the spray stick that did for my brother. It doesn't really matter how he got it. What's important is, here they come, thinking their last little brush with us has opened a chink in our armour."

"I won't tolerate chinks, or any dog-eating persons, inside my armour; especially if they've only got a small brush. Do we get to see hers?"

"The answer is no, Giro. But nevertheless, not to overstretch a metaphorical opening, this is where you could fit in."

"I'm listening, with bartered breath."

"You mean buttered, no doubt. Now, here it is. The next load of drugs from El Queda in Somalia comes over the border into North Kenya pretty soon. Final timing, as usual, to coincide with the shipment of someone's coffin to France, usually some dead holidaymaker. In Kenya, our people will gain access to the coffin at the undertakers, open it up, dump the body and fill the space with poly bags of our white powder. Then at this end, in Nice, backstage at the crematorium, we open the coffin, remove the gear, screw the lid back on again and the cremation of the empty coffin carries on as intended."

"I see, yes, you mean the bags we pack behind the false panels of the Bugatti when you're off round Europe on your vintage car rallies."

"Exactly. Now I've already let them 'intercept' some details about this next shipment in order to lure them in, to let them find out a bit about our Organisation...let them think they're on to us. They'll see what we do all right, they'll get their evidence and we'll swoop, and pop them, bound and gagged, into the coffin we've just opened up and roll it straight down the hatch into the oven. To the hymn tune *Hills of the North Rejoice*, I fancy, if I can find an organist here to play it."

"I'll download it."

"How thoughtful of you, Giro. So like your father. More drink? Yes, but there's been an interesting, not to say arresting, kink in this otherwise seamless garment of a plan."

"Go on. There's many a kink between cuff and the sink. Did not a poet once say that?"

"Not out loud, I shouldn't have thought. Anyway, here's the kink. Not only have they sussed my wheeze, as intended, but they've also made a creditably ingenious counter-plan to avoid being caught and cremated."

"That woman has breasts as credit-worthy as her plans."

"And you'll need considerable ingenuity to get a hold of them, let me tell you. Now, here's what they're going to do...and how we apparently fall for it...but don't. They'll arrange for our hearse to be held up or diverted, by spurious roadworks or something, at some point on its way from Nice airport to the crem. They'll have an exact copy of the coffin to substitute in its place in an identical hearse to ours. But...but...inside it they will have placed, alive and well, if somewhat sexually drained, the bold and brave Dr Strukahrov."

"So, into the back entrance of the crem comes the coffin and we take off the lid to remove the drugs that we expect to find there as usual. But instead, out pops the doctor, armed to the teeth, with Sarin and gas mask. We succumb forthwith and he chops us up, puts us in the coffin, and down through the bake house door...but...."

"She's got a great butt too...."

"It won't be her, it will be him, and anyway there won't be time for consensual sex, even with the likes of you...But...."

"I can't get her butt out of my mind. And so, when the coffin arrives at the crem, we simply bang it straight into the oven without even opening it. Because we know that Russian's in it, and not the drugs."

"What a great mind you have, Giro, if a somewhat lesser behind. We may as well finish the bottle. Cheers. "

"Otherwise, he'd have gassed us."

"Then goosed us, for good measure, who knows?"

"Of our noble bodies he would have made a roast."

"But instead it's the hapless Dr Srukahrof who gets the fry. Waiting in the coffin for his moment of glory, biting his lip, mask and bottle in hand."

"In his hot hand."

"He'll probably scream, being alive in there."

"He might even try and burst the lid off his coffin."

"Not that he could ever get out of the oven."

"We can watch it through the inspection window on the oven door."

"And then maybe send a clip of it to Marina's new mobile. Speaking of which, have you cracked it yet?"

"I thought I had. But it's hardly being used now so I can't be too sure."

"Hope she leaves it on by mistake while it's pointing down

her blouse like the last one."

"You'll be the first to be informed, Branislav."

"I should think so."

ONE TOO FEW AT THE PRIVATE VIEW

ON THE FIRST occasion that the menu button on her new mobile flashed briefly as she disconnected, exactly like the previous one had done, Marina had time for a more leisured response. First, she verified that the pin and name of the potential intruder were the same as before. Then, having thumbed in a cancellation of her new firewall, she got Serena in from a nearby hotel. Neither Branislav nor Girocec had never seen her before because in the course of the last successful hack she was in a public park but behind yesterday's paper.

They put the new mobile on the table, switched it on and, standing in front of it, Serena took off her clothes. Then, using a crimson magic marker, she wrote over the front of her naked body, in mirror image capital letters, next day's date, followed by the address of her hotel, and a time, followed, just above the pubes, with the words "upstairs bar".

And the following evening it dawned on Girocec that if he didn't look out, he was going to come all over his new shirt. This woman was phenomenal...and they were still on the sofa ...and the writing was still on her chest as well as the abdominal wall....

When the coffin came in from Kenya the day after, everything went brilliantly. Except that an unexpectedly quick clearance of the paperwork at Customs meant they had to move the whole thing forward by half an hour and Giro, held up at a meeting, faxed over he couldn't be there to help and sadly, would have to miss the view.

As there could be no delay, for obvious reasons, Branislav got others to help; with accustomed expertise, they had the coffin out of the hearse, onto the trolley, down the rollers and through the oven door in seconds, Slam. Branislav nodded to the cremator who fiddled with some dials and threw a switch.

And much screaming there was. Which came as a shock to the less hardened among them. But none was more shocked nor looked more shaken than Branislav himself, as he spied, through the tiny inspection glass window in the oven door, not the writhing flesh and sinews of Dr Strukahrov, the emigrant and odd physician, but those of his own erstwhile bisexual hardware expert Girocec.

Who had been persuaded, the previous evening, to indulge in a form of literary fore-play and bondage, which, though hardly novel, had kept him tied up all night and the following morning.

Like a half consumed bottle of bubbly, he was not now worth re-corking.

PART 2

A STUMBLE IS ARRANGED

"**Don't give** me any more of your Buddhist crap, Hamish," Hinnie said, wiping her nose with a paper cloth and putting it back in her bag, "What did Buddha ever do for women? Has any Buddhist woman ever reached enlightenment that you actually know of? Never mind what's in books."

Dr Emil Strukahrov, living in a tweed check suit and another assumed name, moved his stool abruptly under the table of the Whole Food café where they'd recently met. This woman obviously had a no mean brain, great bum, plenty of guts and might perhaps be persuaded to join him on the river one evening...but she had just made him feel uneasy...and a bit shivery.

Because he'd once loved a Buddhist nurse, fervently, at least an aspiring one, long ago in an army hospital during the Russian occupation of Afghanistan. It was brief affair, she said she loved him too, but their lives had diverged in the chaos, and talk of Buddhism still clutched at his heart.

Aaagh! There's no going back. Close the door. Don't look back. You're posing as a GP in central Scotland now.

"Hard to say, Hinnie, probably a few. Remind me not to tell you about it if ever I find one. I've often wondered though, d'you think enlightenment can be faked like the female orgasm? I mean, going about smiling serenely all day, doing wonders as a nurse, for example, admired by everyone, but the smile is in anticipation of having sex in the sluice with one of the surgeons, should the opportunity arise."

Which it never did.

Hinnie, being Scorpionic and an expert inquisitor, immediately noted Emil's inner turbulence and pressed on, to see if continued reference to an obviously painful subject might provoke some revealing indiscretion.

"And in their temples, the monks, whatever they are, the

Rinpoches, they're all men as well. That Tibetan place in the Borders is seething with them...what do you call them?...dar-amasallamas."

"Surely that's a form of cod's roe, isn't it?" Emil interrupted in order to change the subject, "my Grannie used to gut them on the Latvian coast."

"You're having me on." Hinnie murmured warmly.

> *Yes, his pupils are constricted. No...they were going both ways. He's on thin ice for sure.*

"Though in fact she was of Scottish descent," Emil continued, somewhat breathlessly, "which was quite possible then and now."

"True enough, Scotland is everywhere."

> *But why would a person of Baltic origin need to be posing as a bearded Scottish country doctor with an interest in karma and re-birth? I think this could be him, that Strukahrov Branislav is after. I'll phone him.*

"I bet you didn't get your feeling for Buddhism down your Grannie's side of the family then," Hinnie said as she got up to go, "knife in hand and bloody apron stained with fish guts."

"No, I got it from a theatre sister I once knew. And it was only a feeling."

> *Is that a joke, or the truth? Enough's enough.*
> *That's sweat beading on his forehead.*

"Going up north for the fishing again tonight?"

Emil nodded.

> *She'd be good in waders, even with*
> *other clothes on as well.*

Outside, Hinnie phoned Branislav.

"I really think it could be him. His family are from the Baltic. He wasn't making that bit up. But he's definitely some kind of fake; on the run or something. His English is sometimes out of an old phrase book. Other bits of his adopted identity don't quite gel either. His medicine sounds kosher all right, but he knows less about Buddhism than my dog, which he strangely resembles."

"He has a lame-dog look?"

"When trying to be sophisticated. It's crazy funny."

"Could well be him. Check with the photo first, then kill him. Whenever...however...and be so good as to send us some tasty snaps of it, if at all possible. As well as copies of the Official Documentation. There's a lot of money hanging on it, Hinnie, ours as well as others, it turns out. Excellent, excellent."

"It's hard to believe he could be a threat. Being such an emotional prat. Was he sent by Putin or just running?"

"On the street though, at his job, he's pretty good. Well trained and still fit. Moscow Special Forces, etc., before legging it to the West, and nobody seems to want to say why. And that means trouble. First the Russians want his head on a spike for what he knows about them in Afghanistan, and now, since he accidentally stumbled into our business, we're out to nail him as well. We got his two girlfriends last year."

"I'll think of something. A final stumble."

"Please do. "

"Something straightforward. perhaps, like into a fresh vat of cement? Or would you prefer it to look more natural; like an unprovoked assault by the Plain Clothes Branch on a cliff top footpath?"

"Hinnie, I leave it up to you, as ever You're the Best. Unmatched. Such a tough nose!"

"It runs in the family."

EMISSION FROM COD

EMIL LIKED nothing more, almost, than the robust to and fro of fruity reminiscence about his student days. A chance meeting with Igor, who'd been a year below him at Brest-Litovsk, soon had their tongues wagging. Especially as it took place on the last train to Inverness and their carriage was otherwise empty.

"...Then there was Nicolai, the thoracic surgeon, remember him?"

"Ward 18. Wee Nick."

"Just a wee nick."

"Blood welling up all over the place."

"The professor would say,' Watch it, Nicolai, careful with the subclavian vein....' Oh Christ Jesus!"

Wee nick, they agreed, always good for a laugh.

"And what about Hughey? 'Where's Hughey?' your mother asked, the morning after the ice-hockey final, 'I heard you all shouting his name last night but he's not come down for his breakfast.'"

"That was Huuughey. Always sick in his bed, that man, could never make it to the pan on time."

"Some of us were doing Huuuccghy all night"

"And Ingrid, the American, the red head...what a...what a... voice."

"Indeed, yes. Ingrid...of the thongs."

"Thighs like the national debt, but they were never parted."

"She parted them on occasions, if not for the likes of us."

"It would've been the Communist Party then."

"Emil, what're you doing? What are you up to these days? That beard is good, but I recognised you straight away."

"General Practice, I catch the last train up to Pitlochry, mid-week, for the fishing, when I get a day off. The train's usually mostly empty like now. And you, Igor, what on earth brings you here? What extraordinary good luck."

"I too am on a kind of mission. A mission, as we used to say in the fishing industry, from cod."

"I sincerely hope you've come better equipped than the last mission we were on together. That weekend in Helsinki after the European championships with only one washable Durex among the three of us."

The train squealed to a halt in the dark, half-way across the Forth Bridge. After several minutes, the conductor came down the carriage holding a briefcase and told them a fire alarm went off and would they move to the front of the train as the carriage they were in would have to be disconnected.

As they passed by an exit door on the side of the train, the conductor, walking behind them, got a steel bar out of his briefcase and brought it down hard on the back of Emil's head with clinical precision. Not too much, nor too little.

While Igor held the unconscious Emil up by his armpits, the conductor unloaded a mass of lead weights from his briefcase into Emil's coat and trouser pockets. Then he pointed an ultra-sonic pen at the control panel beside the exit door, which immediately opened; enabling the two of them, holding an arm and a foot each, to pitch Emil clean out of the train, clear of the spars and struts beside the railway rack, and into the drink down below.

Emil regained consciousness to the sound of the lead weights in his coat and trouser pockets thumping against the raised rivet heads of one of the bridge's giant tubular spars which had broken his fall and down whose curved upper surface he now slithered on his back. Inexorably veering over towards one side of the spar which, because of its curvature, inevitably would dump him into the sea below...unless....

Unless...and he recalled days of a different hue as a student medallist in bob-sleigh and luge...and instinctively rolled his body over, back towards the middle of the spar's curve, pressing down with his arms on the bulky cargo of weights in his pockets for extra leverage as he did so...and it worked...He was still there...At the same time the friction between himself and the rivet heads slowed him down...if he could just stay on long enough....

Ahead, below him, he could make out where the spar he was sliding down butted up against another one at right angles. He cushion his impact against it by bracing his legs and stayed like that for several minutes, curled up in the niche between the two spars like a butterfly in a cocoon, wedged hundreds of feet over the deep, and methodically began to plan his next move.

First, where am I? Answer, left for dead, clearly. Get victim to trust you, sap him and chuck. Make it look like suicide. Who by? Moscow...or...Branislav. Getting Igor onto it was clever. Maybe, he's a shattered ex-army surgeon, the same as me. But getting the conductor involved, and presumably the train driver as well...that smacks of a degree of infiltration...within the community...that's quite beyond Moscow's hit 'n' run mentality. So Branislav's people had finally tracked me down, must be. As if car bombing Marina and Serena last year wasn't enough.

And Hinnie, she must have been in on it as well, as only she knew about these fishing trips. How stupid to get sucked in like that. Never again, he thought, not for the last time. His sense of betrayal warmed him up. Nothing like a murderous grudge to give heat, strength and clarity to a person wedged in mid-air between two giant girders.

So...I'd better stay dead. And let them think mission accomplished. Something of mine will have be found though...yes, this jacket...with my passport in it...and some other items for identification.

He looked around him at the criss-cross geometry of the bridge's construction, and felt entirely at home; reducing the whole thing to a sequence of climbing problems, hand holds, foot holds, etc. First, he took the lead weights from his trouser pockets and dropped them into the sea..

Then, at the first place where he could squat without supporting himself with both hands, he checked his emergency body bag. Found some speed, ate it; found some morphine, injected it; found his mobile wrapped inside a wad of cash, checked both; found his passport, spare house keys and credit cards and put them with his wallet in the inside pocket of his jacket. He then eased his coat off, with its weights, and then his jacket, and let them both go into the sea. With no lead weights in it, the jacket and his identity would soon be washed ashore.

He could see that there was a pub/hotel close to where the

other end of the bridge re-connected with the mainland. And was soon clambering carefully over fences and through back gardens, like a fox, avoiding the road entirely, until he got to the hotel car park. Here, he selected a decent sized modern car, certain to have computerised ignition. Big Stuttgart ones were the best, simple, no longer meant for a prince's stud-farm.

From a choice of several blank keys in his body bag, he found a suitable one for the door lock of a nice juicy Audi and stuck it in...Emil ran the programmable chip embedded in it from his mobile and hacked straight into the car's on-board hard drive. In seconds, a series of numbers popped up on the phone screen which he then typed in...and the car's doors all clicked as they unlocked. A few more numbers released the steering and hand brake and switched on the ignition and the car heater. Audi car heaters were good, except to mechanics.

He got straight onto the northbound M8 and stayed on it till his teeth stopped chattering. He was badly bruised and beaten up. Petrol?...enough. But he couldn't get any more, or do much more, looking like this.

At night, the Special Forces Training Manual said (and still does), that the safest way of getting new clothes is to break into a dry cleaner's in a small town through a back window. Emil kept a length of duct tape in the body bag for this purpose. He covered over the window pane with overlapping strips of it and hit the glass with his fist. Its crack was scarcely audible and, carefully removing the broken glass from the frame, Emil was soon in, small torch between his teeth.

Great...three shirts, two jackets, two trousers and a rain-coat...and small foldable suitcases as well...get one, put the clean clothes in and get out back to car. Back on road, pull off at a remote spot, climb into the back seat and clean up, using torn up old shirt. Put on new gear...comb hair...check for blood...careful round split skin at back of head...clean up shoes as well and get to an all night filling station for petrol and food. Drive on till the morning rush hour...still on speed...abandon car several miles from a large main town, and proceed on foot, carrying bloodstained gear in the folding case, to a big High Street hotel, and check in for a whole week...in the identity of a "recuperating schoolmaster".

OF DEMISE AND MEN

AFTER TWO DAYS, Emil checked out the town's cash dispensers. He had two still unused items in the body bag. A micro-camera the size of a match head and chewing gum. How many times had he practiced this routine during training? First check the location of each bank's CCTV cameras, if any.

At the dispenser booth, he put one hand up to his forehead, legitimately, as if to shield his eyes from the glare of the daylight and thereby get a clearer view of the screen display. Simultaneously he brought his other hand up to his forehead which, shielded from view, deftly and illegitimately stuck a small blob of chewing gum onto the roof of the booth. Embedded in which was the micro-camera, only its lens exposed, and it's micro-innards transmitting directly to Emil's mobile phone.

Standing several yards away from the dispenser, and apparently window shopping, Emil in fact viewed the cash dispenser's keyboard on his phone screen as folk entered their PIN numbers and took their cash. Then he simply had to select someone, a man was always easier, bump into him "by accident", apologising profusely while helping him to his feet and at the same time surreptitiously relieving him of his wallet. Then getting as much cash and goods as possible with it for a couple of hours at the most before chucking the card and getting hold of another one, but only when necessary.

In this way he was soon able to rent to an inconspicuous ground floor bed-sit in a uniform row of similar drab maisonettes in central Glenrothes. From where he planned how he'd stalk Hinnie McHubris and wring her neck till her tongue stuck out, she went blue, shat herself, and died.

A vacant allotment with its own small shed was advertised

at the local post office. Emil obtained the lease and dug a deep pit under the shed for Hinnie's remains, appropriately sized fragments of which he brought to the site in sacks marked "Peat". He then got into her flat with her own keys and made leisurely copies of all the digital data he could find, leaving everything otherwise undisturbed, exactly as he'd found it.

He reckoned he now had about two or three weeks before anybody, including Branislav, would think something was amiss and in that time he would've used the stuff nicked from Hinnie to hack into Branislav's system, and then...mmm...drill him from a distance with a sniper's rifle?

Easy enough but low vengeance rating...a bomb under his Bugatti during a vintage car rally? That would at least even things out for Marina and Serena.

But the main thing, he decided, as it was so personal, and not just professional, was to be there, close up, to witness the brains-out moment or whatever, with absolute certainty. The look on Branislav's face, with Emil grinning at him as his lights went out; that's what counted most for the vengeful emigrant physician, now lurking anonymously in Glenrothes.

DEMISE BY SURPRISE

EMIL, MOSCOW TRAINED, hugely enjoyed unravelling hard drives and the like. A complete portrait of the owner is obtained. Apart from all the e-mails and texts dealing with his arms and drug deals, there was the personal spending as well. In Branislav's case, the clothes, books and CDs, the vintage cars, the villa, the opera, the antiques, the champagne, the sex and other health pursuits. Everything...everything...from his current Viagra requirement to a pair of brand new Danish hearing aids; it was all there. All Emil needed to know about how, why and where Branislav's lifestyle exposed him to risk.

And, with his adversary's intimate cyberspace now in the palm of one hand, Emil busily texted round the world with the other, getting the equipment, renting the van and assembling the perfect murder of his dreams.

A fortnight later at breakfast time, Branislav, in a kitsch cotton dressing gown and matching slippers, was toying with a poached egg in the roof garden of his villa. His egg looked up at him as if it were an evil eye and he seemed, after a few tries, none too keen on having a go at it.

His new physio-therapist came out onto the roof, carrying a tray with champagne glasses and two pills, which she presented to him while sliding naked out of her dressing gown. Branislav downed one of the drinks and both pills and the two of them went indoors, Branislav first removing his two hearing aids and leaving them on the tray.

Emil, in his rented bed-sit in Glenrothes, settled down to wait and watch, noting that the new physio was wearing an identical dressing gown and slippers to her client...Emil took note of Branislav's uneaten breakfast and tasteless bed-ware because he was able to observe the entire roof-top scenario by means of a special Chinese camera installed in an American robotic mini-drone, stolen in Pakistan, re-programmed in Finland and now hovering silently a mile high above the villa. With the rather enterprising and ever resourceful Dr Strukahrov at the controls in Glenrothes, a first for that place.

The drone's unprecedented zoom facility relayed everything, in all its kitsch splendour, onto a 36" wide flat screen monitor in Emil's darkened front room. As much as he liked the big screen, he still had to draw the curtains when the morning sun was low. He could count the ice cubes in Branislav's glass and, with a little more adjustment, could make out the word "Hers" embroidered on the physio's cotton slippers. From his eagle's eye viewpoint, Emil hadn't yet been able to see her face, but the new physio seemed much more mature and grown up than last week's one, more natural, un-posing, relaxed in her nudity as if this was normal...About the same age as himself.

Emil checked and re-checked the drone's electrics on the control panel...and waited. He knew their routine by now. It wouldn't take long. The Viagra was Canadian. The champagne from Rheims.

And sure enough, half an hour later, Branislav came back out into the garden again, put his hearing aids in and began whistling away to the many birds he kept in cages on the roof-top as he topped up their feed trays with little morsels. This was it, Emil decided, there could be no better moment than now; so he flicked the switch on the control panel.

A French radar device in the drone locked onto the specific frequency of the amplified output of Branislav's Danish hearing aids. And this device guided the drone as it raced, at maximum thrust, homing in on the zone between Branislav's two ears. It couldn't miss, there was no dodging it, as no-one could possibly see it or hear it coming.

It was less than half a minute away, on the final, horizontal part of its trajectory, when, completely unexpectedly, the new physio stepped out onto the roof-garden, still naked, except for a light canvas bag on one arm, and began snuggling up to Branislav. Damn. The previous physios all had a shower after, while he fed the pet birds, Would this new physio get out of the drone's path in time?

Otherwise, she'll just have to go with him, Emil decided, and take their matching dressing gowns and slippers with them. Just at that moment he saw, through the drone's lens on the monitor screen in front of him...the look...the very look on Branislav's face that he had wanted...and had waited so long to see...as, turning away from his new physio, Branislav caught sight of a large model jet plane hurtling towards him now at eye level, silently, at greater speed than any drone he'd known.

The new physio hadn't yet seen it. While Branislav's attention was diverted, Emil's monitor displayed her lifting out an antique bayonet from the canvas bag she'd brought into the garden with her and plunging the blade deep into Branislav's left back, in the direction of the heart. She twisted the blade, and left it in.

The initial look of horror on Branislav's face was hurriedly replaced by one of utter disbelief as, in his few remaining sentient moments, Branislav realised that one mode of surprise demise was right behind the other.

As he started to totter due to internal blood loss, it wasn't Branislav's facial expression that occupied Emil's attention so much as the physio-therapist's. She'd clocked for herself the drone's imminent impact; but was standing perfectly still, and smiling serenely, staring fixedly, fearlessly, straight at what was about to destroy her.

Simultaneously, by means of the drone's optics, she was also staring at Emil straight in the face, crouched in front of a giant monitor screen in the front room of his bed-sit in Glenrothes. From where, for the first time, he saw her full in the face, instead of from above.

Who was this woman confronting her fate so unflinchingly, and the emigrant Dr Strukahrov so unknowingly? Where...oh where had he seen her before?

Time stopped.

When it started again, he knew it was Sister Trotskaya. The theatre sister at the army hospital in Kabul. The only nurse he'd met who'd ever asked him if he knew anything about Buddhism, perhaps jokingly he'd first thought, as they gowned up together to get started on the most hellish wounds they'd see that long night.

So the Russians had finally caught up with Branislav as well.

Emil jerked feverishly at the controls to try to activate the drone's manual overdrive in time to save her.

While Sister Trotskaya continued to stare out at him, not batting an eyelid.

> *Work done, the beast is dead. Dad is revenged. I can let*
> *go. Yes. Nothing matters any more. No more hate,*
> *no aversions, no attachments. Yes, I'm ready at long last.*

And she smiled with a serenity that the emigrant Dr Emil

Strukahrov remembered only too well, because it'd once made him feel so grounded, for the first time in his life, and the only time ever since.

The screen went blank. The winter sun went down.

PART 3

OLD BOSHEVIC BLOOD LINE DOWN THE DRAIN

SISTER VERA Natalya Trotskaya, (ex-Soviet operating room nurse and temporary physio-therapist) stood naked in the roof-top garden of her first and last client, her eyes wide open. A robotic mini-drone the size of a large model aeroplane, was headed straight at her, at waist height, barely seconds away, packed with explosives, but, unknown to her, it was being electronically guided to do violence to her companion, the criminal oligarch Branislav, whose own head was at waist height because Sister Vera had just stabbed him in the back and he was expiring on his knees before her.

Little did she know too, or need to, that the drone was controlled from a curtained bed-sit in Glenrothes.

Vera Natalya's mother, the illegitimate child of a murdered Bolshevic military genius, had always re-assured the family that there was no visible pain at all for the victim in any of the deaths by firing squad that she'd witnessed in the camps.

As countless life-times swam in and out of her view, Vera Natalya had a vision of her grandparents in the bullet strewn streets of St Petersburg in the first full flood tide of their relationship...when suddenly the drone swerved off course, banking sharply, and went straight through the doorway leading off the roof into Branislav's master bedroom, breaking off its wings as it did so.

Which separated the detonator in the main body of the drone from the explosives in its wings. Meaning that the wingless fuselage, though causing irreparable damage to a priceless Louis Quinze fireplace on the opposite wall, didn't set the whole place on fire.

Hearing the explosion within Branislav's bedroom, which she had only just herself vacated, Sister Trotskaya came back into the moment in a second, and leaving her ersrtwhile client gasping on the roof-top floor, hurried indoors and searched

140

among the debris to see if she could retrieve her clothing...and then stopped. Someone else in the villa, she thought, is sure to be hurrying upstairs to see what's happened. Without hesitation she went back onto the roof and withdrew the antique bayonet from Branislav's not yet quite dead back. Then, rolling him over to and fro, she removed his light linen jacket, cotton shirt, trousers, and espadrilles and put them on herself.

Then she leaped a flimsy low wooden-fence wall out onto the roof's edge. Where she saw the gutters collecting rainwater off the roof garden emptied into one main pipe that went all the way to the ground. Down it she slid, making as little mess as possible of the now deceased Branislav's jacket and trousers, and hailed a taxi.

NO GOING BACK TO GLENROTHES

THE DUTY CLERKESS at the front desk of the Ukranian consulate in Nice replied to Vera Natalya's coded introduction by lifting a red phone, speaking briefly and then asking the ex-army nurse, (and now retired physiotherapist) to kindly step this way. The Consul General at the other end of the red phone picked up a green one and told the second consul to warm up the third Mercedes for an imminent departure.

In Glenrothes, an emotionally drained Dr Emil Strukahrov switched off the monitor screen and packed it, with all the rest of drone's guidance equipment, into sacks marked "Peat" and the next day took them to his nearby allotment and buried them in a pit underneath the floor of its shed, alongside the bagged remains of other nefarious activities that the endlessly emigrant physician had recently had to practice. To this foul gubbins, in its under-shed tomb, Emil now added the optical-electric control system of the missile that he wrongly assumed had just vapourised the only woman ever to have said that she loved him.

He replaced the trap door over the pit entrance, stamped down the earth between it and the wooden slats of the floor of the shed and with a heavy heart, spare clothes and emergency body bag got a taxi to Glenrothes railway station where he left the country, again under an assumed name.

To try once more, and once more only, to escape from his past, and live his future in the present with the same calm steadiness and detachment he had seen in the eyes his now lost love in those last few moments before she'd perished by his own hand. It was a tall order, even for someone with a better grasp of common English usage than himself.

He licked his fingers and tried to flatten down the front of his hair. On a bad hair days like these, his quiff stuck up a mile and made him look ridiculous.

"What do you smile about?" he'd once asked Sister Trotskaya, in the old days, while scrubbing up for another operation, both of them half dead with exhaustion, "Are you laughing at my quif?"

"No, she said. "I like it. It's so you. It sticks up because it's brave and resourceful in the face of almost anything, like you. I'm smiling because I know I love you for that, Emil." She paused to dry her hands. "Emil, do you believe in re-birth?"

"I've read about it and I'd like to believe in it. But if it's true, then I wouldn't want another life like this, Vera Natalya, that is, up to now I mean, up to these days, if you see what I mean, being here with you, like we are now...even though we're up to our necks in shite. Its beginning to feel as if we're becoming one person. I've never known anything like it."

"Nor me. Exactly. I feel so secure about it. It's what makes me feel we've known each other intimately for years in a past life."

"If it was that good then, like now, then why all this blood and guts, Natalya. Why do we have to go through all this...this... to get together again. What could we have done, in our past life together, to deserve all this fucking suffering day and night?"

"It's isn't what we want, but perhaps its what we need."

"You mean Kabul, tonight, is kind of divine blow-lamp sent

down like lightning to weld us together?"

"Keep God out of it, Emil. It's down to us."

"You mean up, surely."

Bells rang, Stretchers came off trucks, most of them with sheets pulled up over dead faces. With fewer operations, there might have been time for more re-weld later. But there wasn't.

Now other bells rang, other whistles blew and another train squealed to a halt. This one the last in a long sequence taking Emil and his grief to India where he sat on a bench in the main station concourse, heaving with tears, and tried to drink some bottled water. Eventually he ate a banana, carelessly chucking the peel backwards over his shoulder. Something made him turn round. In surprise he saw its possession contested by two rats. The winner's tail flicked a few times as it made off with the prize immediately.

But not being able to see where it was going with the peel over its head, the rat ran straight into a wall. The peel fell and the other rat made off with it. The first rat, wobbling, slightly stunned, came to its senses and went in the opposite direction, without contesting the peel any further.

Not unlike my own shit hole of a so-called life, mused the emigrant physician, and in the process found himself ekeing out the semblance of a small smile, the first for weeks, in sympathy with his ratty counterpart. He had to abandon this fucked up "peel", or husk of an "outer self" that had resulted in his getting banged up so often...and leave it to the rats here and now. He sat up straight...no going back...so right dad...and then felt two hands being placed over his eyes, from behind.

"Don't Move. Guess who?"

He guessed immediately from the sound of the voice and froze in fright and disbelief.

143

OLD BLADES IN SAFE HOUSES

"**WELL THEN,**" the Consul General purred, warming to the occasion after the briefest of de-briefings and pouring out the coffee himself, "tell me, in strictest confidence of course, am I or am I not talking to a woman illegitimately descended from my great personal hero; the man who forged the Red army, Leon Trotsky, Internationalist and Permanent Rebel?" The Consul General's family were experienced rug dealers from around the north coast of the Black Sea near where Trotsky was born.

"Don't talk such nonsense, especially such amusing nonsense," Vera Natalya replied, restored to a neat tweed skirt, as well as the proverbial acerbic wit of her alleged forbear.

"Though the myth needs up-dating," she went on. "Whose was the last secret blood line to be made into a successful film? Was it Leonardo da Vinci or Jesus Christ, I can't remember. Imagine the headlines,

"Stark tale involving daughter of Trotsky's secret love-child." "Narrow escape from being impaled by drone," the Consul General continued, something of a dabbler in pulp fiction himself. "On the rooftop of a gangster's villa who had tortured and murdered her father."

"We shouldn't overcook it. Too Dostoevsky. It would make more sense for you to be descended down a secret blood line from Vlad the Impaler."

Indeed, Sister Trotskaya decided, with his long nose, handle bar moustache and piercing eyes, the Consul General strongly resembled depictions of that monster, as he smirked in an oily way over the coffee; trying at the same time to figure out what to do with her next.

She would certainly get a huge reward for eliminating Branislav; Dacha by the sea, that sort of thing, as well as a life long bodyguard. After all, she'd just eliminated public enemy No. 1 for the underhand sales of arms, as well as kidneys and other body parts, to the losers as well as the winners of the last

"Gaberdine Revolution" in the Ukraine. His killer was one hot potato.

"I think it best we get you back to Kiev, and into the hands of the new Secretary of State for Home Affairs."

Little or no chance of a shag here at all.

"We can soon get you out of the country in complete safety, tucked in the diplomatic bag as it were, beside me in the back seat of the Mercedes. Then it'll be up to you. Anything you need in the immediate future?"

"Look, your excellency," Sister Trotskaya stood up, "What I want is a Tibetan monastery. To be taken there, left at the gate, learn how to meditate and die."

What a great idea, Get her off my hands altogether and on the cheap too. But...hmmm...problems... don't contradict her though.

"I'll see to it. Easy enough, from our point of view. But at the present time, western women look a little suspicious outside temple gates and you'd be immediately picked up by Chinese secret police. Which would lead them to us. Why not meditate in a Tibetan refugee camp on the Indian side of the border where there's hundreds of other devotees like your good self with whom you could inconspicuously mingle, without a bodyguard."

"How long would it take?"

"What, to die of meditation? I've no idea. It would depend on what they gave you to eat. Then there's malaria, the runs... and so forth."

"No, no, no, your excellency, how long before you can get me out of here?"

"No time at all" He drummed his fingers on the low coffee table, narrowed his options and widened his horizons. "And... and...assuming you're warm and dry, what on earth do you think about when you're meditating all day?"

"You try and empty your mind of all the rubbish normally

prancing around inside it. You try not think about anything."

"Quite."

"But trains come into the station. Trains of thought."

"Naturally."

"But you don't have to get on board any of those trains."

"Of course not, no."

"And if you do, then you certainly don't have to clean out the toilets."

She seems to have read my mind.

"I should think not. No. I agree. Yes. I can see what you're driving at."

"And, after a while, trains will leave the station."

"Yes, what a relief that must be. But one is still left waiting for the next train of thought to come into the station, is one not? This one being that, sooner or later one is going to have to start begging again, not least or one's dinner."

"Maybe, but not necessarily expecting any. Not attached to the idea of getting some. Eventually, without any attachments of any kind, there can be no disappointment if what you expect or hope for doesn't show up."

This was where the Consul General usually lost his place; when the discussion came down to attachments. To him and his family, in the rug trade, an attachment is what you put onto the end of your vacuum cleaner to get fluff and food remains out of those awkward corners. One simply can't do without them. One has to be practical.

"I'll get things going right away. You'll need health checks, inoculations, papers, etc. Get them in Kiev, then take them to our Embassy in New Delhi and acclimatise. Get some simple clothing. Then make your way north to the Tibetan border. Should take about three weeks on foot. What about the last of the coffee? Good, isn't it. Italian of course. By the way it's full blown ambassadors who get addressed as Your Excellency. Not mere Consul Generals like myself from the next drawer down."

As they were leaving the room, he chortled "Can I interest

you in anything for the weekend then? But, of course, I keep forgetting, you're now officially retired from physical-therapies."

"Watch it, your worship. This may be a safe house, and I'll get my corset suitably modified to accommodate another antique blade, but it won't include yours. Though I'll speak very well of your kindness and efficiency and fine coffee to my cousin, the next Secretary of State for Home Affairs."

"Whatever do you mean?"

"When the new day dawns, on the next night of the long knives."

"I see. Not too soon, I trust, and hopefully not before you've got yourself some long trousers."

> *So like her alleged grandfather, it's uncanny! It has to be her in spite of her witty denial. Very dangerous for all concerned if it were ever genetically proven. So many of Trotsky's family and entourage were also assassinated.*

A SACRED LUNCH IS SERVED

NO SOONER had Sister Trotskaya, in a plain hijab as advised, waved goodbye to her escort at the station in New Delhi, when, to her great surprise, she saw in the distance, sitting on a bench on the main concourse and chewing a banana, someone looking distinctly like a surgeon she'd once fallen in love with at the military hospital in Kabul. Years and years ago now. Could it possibly be him? It was. She got nearer to make sure. He hadn't changed much. That quiff was unmistakable, even at a distance, no matter how hard he tried to smarm it down with his fingers. She came right behind him and put her hands over his eyes

"Sister Trotskaya, there's no-one alive on earth with sweet hands like yours and a voice to match. Am I right?"

If wrong, he thought, this is the warm up to an almost certain abduction, hammering and death. Fuck. Like so many times before. It was always the same...the initial act of affection to put you off your guard...the light at the end of the tunnel...

147

attached to an on-coming train. Fuck Fuck Fuck!

"Emil, Emil, Emil!" she couldn't let go of him. And when she did, her fingers were soaked with his tears. "Oh Emil."

She leaned her head against the back of his neck and he smelt phenomenal. First the heat of arousal, then relief that the manual override on the drone had worked, all mingled with cold sweat and fear.

How could she have found me, who's sent her
after me and why?

He'd never know now. This was the end of the road. He was too tired and waited with acceptance for the axe to fall, the blade's scratch on his neck.

She kissed his neck and ears, and ran her hands through his hair. He reached up with his own hands, to try and prevent her killing him so soon.

The two of them stayed like this for so long that a passing sacred cow put its snout in Emil's opened back pack and trotted off with his last two somozas.

SISTER TROTSKAYA'S APPENDIX

AND OVER the next days and weeks they slept on pavements alongside rickshaw drivers. and felt as warm and safe as they'd ever been. Slowly they began to assemble for each other, piece by piece, the jig-saw puzzles of their separate lives. Emil looked blissfully happy. It was for this very reason, one night, that Sister Trotskaya decided it was time to go. She looked over at the sleeping face of her lover and tore an empty page from the back of a book the Nice Consul General had given her to write something down. Something she could leave for him, to help him understand.

"Emil, I'm going. I have to. Don't try and follow me or find me. A stage in our lives has been played out. It's over now and by the time you read this I'll be gone. I can feel the warmth of your attachment even now. And that's the trouble, Emil, it's what I want, but I have to recognise it's no longer what I need for the next stage. And so must you, Emil. We both need non-attachment now. Thank you so very much for giving me the resources, over these past weeks to have a proper shot at it, at last. Don't get angry with me or with yourself. Your quiff will get rigid and catch fire. To prevent this happening and spoiling your beautiful shining features, I'm removing some for safe keeping."

She reached over towards him and with the scissors of her Swiss army knife, cut a piece off the front of his hair, and put it between two Kleenex tissues inside the book. Immediately she thought of something else she wanted to add. Damn, she was going to need more paper. She found one of the Consul General's calling cards at the bottom of her back-pack and inked out the printed side. On the back she wrote:

"Christ this is the hard bit. Goodbye Emil, I'm going now. Fare the well sweet one. And thanks once more. Keep smiling, for both of us. Till the next life then.

All things have their season. It comes, they go, that's all.
Does Summer mourn the Springtime rain? Does Winter grieve
the Fall?
Does the sea-bird, soaring up high, look back to the shore?
So I've put your quiff in a handkerchief, to keep its curvature."

PART 4.

THE THIN CARD AND THE FAT PULP NOVELLA

WITH SHREWD PROFESSIONAL INTEREST, the First Secretary at the Ukranian Embassy in New Delhi surveyed the scruffy yet otherwise clean enough looking man with well oiled hair standing in front of her.

A few minutes ago, he'd presented himself to the clerk at the front desk in the embassy foyer without an appointment seeking assistance to trace the whereabouts of a missing person, his close friend, of Ukranian origen, who'd mysteriously vanished, without trace, except for one small thing which she'd left behind. A calling card, that looked as if it had been soaked in the monsoon and then dried out, but the imprinted crest of the Ukranian National coat of arms was clearly visible. But the desk clerk smelt a rat, as he had been trained to do in the Secret Service; and rats were a matter for the First Secretary who was also in Secret Service and had only recently been promoted from the front desk at the Consulate in Nice.

The new First Secretary came down to the embassy foyer and could see at once that the card was the real thing, because the name and telephone number printed below the coat of arms were well known to her, being a code. With the result that she did exactly the same thing that she'd done when first confronted with this code, orally, during her days in Nice, and asked the man with the frayed card if he'd kindly step this way, nodding with approval at the front desk clerk for his ratty perspicacity.

"Where and how did you get this?" asked the First Secretary, once behind the closed door of her office. while the device incorporated into the door scanned the man's entire body for concealed weaponry.

The emigrant Dr Emil Strukahrov had carefully considered his reply to this in the rickshaw on the way to the Embassy. Not too much, not too little. He aimed to be passed swiftly on up to the next spook in the ladder, hopefully to the Ambassador.

"My friend left it behind", he said, and paused in sadness, "the only thing she left behind when she disappeared...without any warning, vanished, fucked off...I don't know where, I want to find her."

Not too angry now. Vera Natalya did tell me.

"Could you possibly let me have closer look at it?"

"No. I don't want anybody I can't trust to touch it. I might not get it back."

"Perfectly understandable. Could you perhaps place it on the desk then, so I can examine it a little better, hands behind my back, without there being any danger of your losing possession of it?"

"Of course."

Keep head bent forwards over it to shield it from any camera hidden in the ceiling directly overhead.

"Yes, indeed, I can see that this card is....could...be...er...very helpful in your search."

Clever boy. But he won't know we've now got our cameras in earrings.

The new First Secretary found it hard to conceal her astonishment, as the coded phone number on the card was the same as that given to her by that bedraggled woman, Trotskaya, at the front desk of the Consulate in Nice a few months ago, just after having murdered some notorious gangster. Then, as now, this was red phone event.

"Ambassador? Have you a spare moment please?"

His Excellency. only recently promoted to the top drawer himself, from having been a mere Consul General in Nice, said he did. One simply had to have spare moments for the red phone, in fact and in fiction. An example of the latter, a short pulp espionage story, was open on his desk.

"I've got someone with me in the office, sir, who's recently come into the possession of a rather unique object which both he and I agree might well be of some importance."

151

"Yes, what"?

"It's a calling card, sir. With our national crest on it, bearing the name Victor Serapian. And underneath it a printed a telephone number..." which the upgraded First Secretary read out slowly, "Does it ring a bell, sir?"

His recently promoted Excellency, somewhat alarmed, agreed that it did. Victor Serapian was not his name, but he was well aware that the telephone number was code, because he had created it himself. So could the First Secretary bring the man up, having made sure she'd secretly got a photo of the card first? She had. And was the man armed? He wasn't. But would she alert the office of the Military Attache anyway? She did.

His Excellency put the red phone down and activated a mini-camcorder installed in the lampshade of a reading light on his desk. Another camera covered the entire stairway leading to his office was on the whole time. He opened his lap top to view it.

What on earth can have happened to that Trotskaya woman, he wondered, and who is this spiv with the smarmy hair coming up the stairs? What possible connection can he have had to her? What's he up to? Probably raped and murdered her and out for some blackmail I suppose. Going to have to be extremely careful here. He closed the well thumbed pulp novella on his desk and put it in his jacket pocket.

GOODBYE TO THE BACK-PACK GHETTO IN THE SKY

SISTER TROTSKAYA, Emil's quiff freshly flattened between the pages of her book, caught the first train that night from New Delhi going north. By the time of its arrival at the railhead in the morning, she realised that most of the passengers were backpackers very like herself. mainly Europeans; except that, in conversation with them, they mostly seemed to be refugees from more existential and less bloodstained perils than hers.

She was told a bus from the station could take her up to a town high in the hills, and the Tibetan temple complex there.

152

Long established, with lots of accommodation in a nearby town.

So far so good, she thought.

But after about a week, it occurred to Sister Trotskaya that she hadn't come all this way to meditate and die in what amounted to a backpackers' ghetto. So she caught the bus back to the railway station and had some chai, complementing the vendor on its quality. He told her that he'd a twin brother who lived near a similar Tibetan Temple/refugee-centre hundreds of miles away in the south, far from any spiritual tourists, where AI and Big Data hadn't been imported yet, and the cloud was yet to come.

"Boil-in-a-bag Buddhists, those tourists," Sister Trotskaya said, quoting something she'd read.

"Thieves and vagabonds part them from their money."

"So true and how easily. Do you think I'll find your brother?"

"As he looks exactly like me, there'll no mistaking him at the bus station there. He also sells chai. The black tea is so much better than up here. Tell him Pandit Nehru sends his best wishes. It's a family joke. He'll introduce you to our Mother."

Natalya was well accustomed to arduous long distance travel. The quiff-stiffened kleenex tissues made a good marker in the Buddhist booklet "Taming the Tiger" that the Consul General had given her in Nice.

"*THE WAY BEYOND SUFFERING LIES IN THE DEVELOPMENT OF FRIENDSHIP WITHIN OUR FAMILIES, OUR SOCIETY AND BETWEEN NATIONS EVERYWHERE ELSE.*"

Natalya bent over the corner of the page this was on, to be able to find it again. When she stopped reading, she placed the marker in its new place. She loved the smell of India; it was hard to put it out of mind, especially when you're supposed to be meditating.

THE FRONT DESK OF THE NEXT LIFE

AFTER DISCOVERING Vera Natalya's goodbye note beside him, Emil went completely numb, withdrawn and unresponsive. His quiff, as forecast, would've stood on end for weeks, had it not been excised, for safe keeping by Vera Natalya herself in her very last moment with him.

The two of them had made themselves well known and respected members of an informal commune of rickshaw drivers centered in New Delhi's main railway station. Both could cook, make chai, and were quick to learn languages, and both were useful in an on-street business renovating rickshaws and the motorised scooter-taxis that clattered about non-stop.

Their new friends realised what had happened to Emil, and continued to share food with him as he sat about in solitary silence. In turn he now noticed that rickshaw drivers didn't seem to meditate very much, if at all, yet they managed to co-exist peacefully in a co-operative and caring community, even though, certainly, there were villains amongst them, controlling many little businesses ruthlessly like petty monarchs, allocating the best pitches by means of bribes they called insurance.

Emil spent long hours on the very bench where he and Vera Natalya had re-discovered each other; chucking banana peels, as well as the entire uneaten fruit to the rats, and then looking on to see what happened. The same thing as before, usually. Vicious competition for the prize. The rats seldom attacked and ate each other though, like we do. At least not in public. Emil remained essentially, if not romantically, realistic.

He missed his quiff more than he thought he would. Licking his fingers and running them through his hair, as Vera Natalya used to do for hours on end, wasn't the same on his own, especially with no quiff left to speak of. "What did she think she was up to?" he wondered one day, as a pair of rats scuttled by, one stopping to pick up a peanut, "going on about having no attachments, when she was just about to detach my quiff and then attach it to herself, albeit between Kleenex tissues in a book?"

On impulse he recovered, from the depths of his body belt,

the card on which she'd written, at the last moment, four lines of heart breaking poetry about the need to cast loose attachments: "All things have their season..." As he stared at this now somewhat battered relic in his hand, he noticed that on the other side of it, carefully, but not carefully enough inked out, was a printed name and address, just visible.

As instructed in the Special Forces Manual, discontinued recently, he held the card flat between the forefinger and thumb of one hand and gently dripped a little bottled water over it with the other, tilting the card to and fro, so that the water covered the card thinly and evenly as it was allowed to drain off; removing with it some ink that had dissolved in it. After a few more tries, the Ukranian National coat of arms showed itself with the address of the Ukranian Consulate in Nice and a name and telephone number underneath it.

The card, unknown to Emil, was given to Sister Trotskaya long before they'd re-met, by the then Consul General in Nice himself. Telling her that the name and telephone number were fictitious, a code by which the Consul General could be contacted, in the strictest confidence on a 24/7 basis year round.

And she had forgotten about this seemingly trivial item, believing it to be merely the parting shot of a man, albeit a well connected one, hoping thereby to put his marker down for a future shag.

Emil had no idea of the card's origin but nevertheless knew exactly what he'd do with it. He dried it off carefully between tissues and got one of his new friends, who was delighted to see a glint in his companion's eye once more, to rickshaw him to the Ukranian Embassy, as faraway as it might happen to be.

Whistles blew. Bells rang and another train pulled into the station, squealing to a halt, Emil cleaned his face, carefully oiled and combed his long thick black hair and strode with renewed confidence up to the bullet-proof screen in front of the highly polished front desk of his Next Life.

"**THE FIRST THING** we need to know," the Ukranian Ambassador said, "obviously, in order to assist you with your search, is this. Exactly how did you obtain this card?"

"Yes."

"Go on"

"It's a long story."

"Very likely. Let's have a cup of coffee while we're at it then. Will you see to it, Irina?" The First Secretary went down to the kitchen and made the coffee herself, placing on the tray, besides the set of cups and saucers specially coated to pick up finger-prints, a generous supply of chocolate biscuits.

"It's very good coffee, Italian," purred the Ambassador, while waiting.

"They had the same in the Nice Consulate as well, so my friend once said."

Ye Gods, there's very few who would know this.

It could tie him in. Still, could have murdered her.

"When was that?"

"While she was in the consulate there. A lot had happened to us before that. Perhaps I should begin at the beginning."

The First Secretary came in with the tray. Dr Strukahrov began his narrative in Afghanistan. An hour later the coffee and biscuits were finished and the First Secretary removed the tray. Lunch was brought in on another. Dr Strukahrov's fingerprints on his cup and saucer were scanned and filed.

The Ambassador was enjoying himself.

This is some of the best pulp I've ever heard in my life. Utterly explosive. Even if it's all untrue, it's a cracking good yarn, as the British Ambassador was wont to say at tea parties.

"The French Authorities never found out who made that drone or why."

"I can help you with that."

"Really?"

"Because it was me."

"You?"

> *Dynamite. What an unexpected twist.*
> *Thank God the recorder's still running.*

"Yes"

"Why?"

"It'll take some explaining. It's another story altogether, un-related."

"We'd better get the cognac out then, would you Irina." The First Secretary did.

Dr Strukahrov needed to go to the toilet. His Excellency confided with Irina.

"First things first. Get started on whatever's necessary to get him Political Asylum here. We can't let him go with what he appears to know. But to establish his identity, the puzzle needs three more pieces. First, we need to match his fingerprints with any the French may have found on what was left of that drone. Break in to Police headquarters in Nice. The security was never too great in that building. Window locks defective. Filing cabinets not secure, etc. "

"Will do."

"The next piece is Sister Trotskaya herself. Establish her whereabouts."

"We should have tagged her."

"I discussed this with her cousin. He said she really did want to vanish completely, entirely. Sever all attachments. And that we should let her go, honour her intentions."

There was a pause.

"And the third piece, Your Excellency?"

"Well, it's less in connection with Strukahrov's exact identity and more to do with the book I'm thinking of writing about these extraordinary adventures. It'll need absolute positive proof of the Trotsky blood-line though, if I want this to sell, under an assumed name of course, when I retire. Sister Trot-skaya would obviously need to be involved."

Dr Strukahrov returned from the toilet. More cognac was had.

"With that unusual name she had, did the subject, much rumoured, of Trotsky having a secret love-child ever arise, and that she might be his grand-daughter? Did this subject crop up while you two were down and out amongst the rickshaws or up to your necks in surgical gowns?"

"It did. She was certain about it. Her father had told her, he even knew where the ice pick actually used to kill Trotsky could be found. After the trial of the assassin, it was handed over to Trotsky's second wife and family who were living with him in Mexico at the time."

"What on earth did they do with it?"

"All her father knew was that it was said to have ended up under the bed of one of Trotsky's sons."

"Under the bed?"

> Christ. First this affair was going to be a pulp novella, now it's turned into a bedroom farce. Better cut this Strukahrov in on the action right away. With his knowledge of the Special Forces Manual, not to mention his own life's trajectory, the doctor would make a perfect Technical Adviser for the book while in residence here. Get the First Secretary in on it as well as Co-author. Her cyber-electronics might be more up to date than his, and she can prepare the drafts as well as keep them securely locked away.

His Excellency put his fictional cards on the table. Game, match, and pulp novella were on, without demur, especially for Emil who could see that he'd now become, for the first time ever in his life, the rat with the nut between his teeth.

The First Secretary got out a new exercise book, and asked how they could possibly get their hands on Sister Trotskaya's DNA profile to start with. Emil, in his element, said that blood would have taken for health checks while in Kiev, before she went on to New Delhi.

"You'd need her cousin's consent to get the DNA looked at," said the Technical Advisor. "They're both very sensitive about this issue. He'd take persuading. No gain at all for either of them. They don't need money. And a break-in is out of the question."

Emil went on, "It's occurred to me that she must've scraped herself sliding down that drainpipe. And what happened to Branislav's jacket and trousers? There could be traces of her blood on it, at the sleeves and cuffs."

The Principal Author, while still a Consul General, had himself poly-bagged them when he got Sister Trotskaya a smart new tweed suit in Nice. And had brought these clothes with him in the...ahem...diplomatic bag, when he was transferred to New Delhi. He hadn't wanted the French Police to lay their hands on them, nor his successor as Consul General in Nice. "There was blood on the jacket all right but we assumed it was all Branislav's and never thought to get it checked out. Sound thinking, Strukahrov. Let's see to that, Irina."

"Next, we get under the bed, looking for the ice-pick," the Technical Adviser said.

"Indeed we shall. How, again, did it get there?"

"One of Trotsky's sons used to brag about it when drunk. Trotsky's family returned to the Ukraine where Vera Natalya's father had always lived. He knew of the family but kept his distance. So many had been murdered. This particular son, as a boy, was the first person to arrive at the crime scene, just back home from school, to discover his father bleeding to death on the floor carpet and that Stalinist swine standing over him with the ice-pick."

"Bleeding on the carpet, did I hear you say?"

Cue lights. Cue trombones. A good place, in the opera for a quartet, including Trotsky's secretary, off-stage, who the assassin was shagging on the side in order to gain access to the family household. Unbeatable!

159

"Profusely. The whole place is now a museum and Trotsky's study is preserved exactly as it was on the day. So she said."

"Even the carpet. Still there?"

"Who knows".

"Was it ever cleaned?"

"Ditto, Your Eggsellency. This cognac's very good."

"And the ice pick, therefore, could also have Trotsky's blood on it."

"It did, so Vera Natalya's father was told."

"And where is it...this bed...and this son...is he still alive?"

Will anybody believe the half of all this,
even if it all turns out to be true?

"Voklov was his name," said the Technical Advisor.

"Then we can easily trace him," said the Co-author, "easily."

"Yes, and get under his bed pronto, while he's down at the boozer, and if the ice-pick's still there and there's still blood-stains, use a moist hydroid gel swab, to get some of it off for DNA analysis."

You don't have to tell me how to do anything, thought this Co-author, a highly trained behind-the-scenes operative in her own right. Things have moved on since your day, chummy, and the book's not going to read like an American Western or some other Schlockian out of Michigan either.

"Leave the pick under the bed after so's he won't know what's been done," the Technical Advisor further advised.

He's on the ball though, the Co-author had to admit. "Your Excellency," she went on, "It might be worth trying the museum in Mexico as well."

"You mean remove bits off the pile of that carpet. I hadn't thought of that," said the Technical Adviser.

"While the museum is closed for necessary refurbishment," chimed in the well connected Principal Author and Diplomat of some Influence, "for which we will furnish necessary funds."

"And of course," he went on, catching up with the chase, "if there was that much blood on it when Trotsky died, there might well still be some left, albeit dried out, waiting for us."

"It will take me a bit of doing," said the Technical Advisor, "to pull off both jobs, Your Excellency, even with your people doing the back-up. I'm not getting any younger you know, but if you can't find anybody else...."

Don't look at me, blinked the First Secretary as His Excellency's gaze wandered her way. This mission was desperately tricky and she'd definitely have preferred to remain in New Delhi as Co-author.

"No, of course not. Emil, yes. May I call you Emil?" asked the Principal Author, "it was never our intention...much too risky for you, and all of us here for that matter, if anything went wrong. I'll see to everything. Mossad does this sort of thing to perfection. After all Trotsky came from a Jewish family and it'll put one up the noses of those Russkies. First Secretary, are the papers ready?"

"They are, Your Excellency."

"Good. Right then, Emil, it's all fixed up. While we attend to these matters, you reside here safe and sound, in Political Asylum, on the sidelines, for once, with your very own room, for visiting VIPs, above me on the fourth floor. All meals brought in, except the ones we share while we attend to finding your missing person; and ours now, as it turns out. This will be more difficult than anything else."

> *Apart from trying to put together a meaningfully thrilling novella about it at the same time. With all the new love interest injected into it that we didn't know about, before, it's shaping up to be a real cracker.*

"There's wan thing I'm not too 'appy about," said Dr Strukahrov with a slight slur, "is this. If we get the whole love-blood-child-line thing no...sorry...this love-child-blood-line thing... sorted, I don't think she'll wanna know about it. Or be even innerested. She, her cousin and ourselves, we believe we know who she is. Maybe we should leave it at that. The publicity, neither o'them would ever (hic)...wannit."

The Co-author had considered this, "Why not keep the plot, in all its juicy detail, but change all the characters' names and the places where the story is set. To protect the innocent."

"But there aren't any," His Excellency said, "Even in real life," he added, looking in the general direction of the Technical Adviser, a self-admitted killer and DIY cremator, who nodded in agreement.

"Except Vera Natalya, herself" Emil added.

"Exactly, that's the trouble with our book", said its new Co-author. "So why not set it in Scotland instead? Emil can advise on the scenery and the weather as well as giving the plot any appropriate local colour."

"I could indeed," said the Technical Adviser, and from what little I've learned about Scottish Culture, it would be better to turn the whole thing into a saga about the secret blood line of a martyred unsung poet."

The cognac finished, Emil went to his bed and the other two about their respective business.

FALL-OUT FROM TAMING THE TIGER

"PANDIT NEHRU sends his best wishes. He says your chai is better than his, thanks to the different black tea you have down here," Vera Natalya said, glad to have arrived in Namdroling, among fragrant Sandal trees of South India.

"And better cardamoms too," said the twin brother of the chai vendor she'd met in the hills up north. Who had recommended his brother and told her how he usually journeyed to Bangalore himself, on the roof of overcrowded buses, returning home for festivals and family events.

"And how long you let it all simmer, before adding the milk and sugar and boiling everything again."

This went on for some time. Vera Natalya could hold her own on the food and drink front with all-comers.

And as predicted, she soon found herself sitting on the floor opposite the chai twins' mother. What wasn't included in the prediction was that this would be in the company of others in the extended family, and some of her neighbours as well, meditating as a group, One of whom had a spare room. Everything tastes and smells so different in Southern India. Her senses overwhelmed her. This wasn't trains of mad monkey thought racing into the station...it was horses...bolting...wild horses...of feeling...sensation...every time...she breathed in.

In the book she had with her, *Taming the Tiger*, a present from His Excellency with its blank page torn out, it said, "TO TAME EITHER A HORSE, OR OUR MIND, WE MUST FIRST MAKE FRIENDS WITH IT."

The paper book mark and its quiff had stayed on this page for days before being moved on.

"INSTEAD OF SHUNNING THE PLAY OF THE MIND," the words at the next quiff-stop read, "TRY TO RELAX, OBSERVE AND FIND THE WAY IN." She'd dropped a little sandalwood oil on the tissues comprising the bookmark. Wherever it was parked, it lent its perfume to the page and, increasingly, to the tuft of hair between the tissues of the bookmark, and to her fingers.

One evening, after a long walk, she came back to find the house where she was living ransacked. All the rooms done over, taking away money, mobile phones, computers. Vera's rucksack was gone and everything in it, except the Consul General's book, which had been searched for paper money and then thrown away. The bookmark and its enclosed tuft of hair were now lost, indistinguishable from the general debris, much of it smashed up, as if in a frenzy. The family were distraught. She helped them clear up and sat with them and other neighbours in a group meditation. The mother of the two twins held a book in her hands and quoted from it without bothering to look down at the page. It was written by the same Precious One, that wrote the book the Consul General had given her in Nice:

"WE HAVE TO ACCEPT THE LIMITATIONS OF BEING HUMAN.
ALLOW NEGATIVE THOUGHTS TO FLOW THROUGH US WITHOUT

After, everyone agreed with Vera Natalya that the ransacking
was a clear signal, it was time for her to continue her journey,
having taken detachment and inactivity as far as she could. The
following day, in new clothes and enough cash in her body belt
for a few days, she walked to the nearest bus station and into
her next life, pulling a new small suitcase on wheels behind her.

A BELLY-FULL OF ATTACHMENTS

A MONTH AFTER the last Ambassadorial writers' conference, His
Excellency had attended to all the various matters discussed between himself, his Co-author and the Technical Adviser when
the red phone rang on his desk, yet again.

No, no, not again.

"Yes?"

"It's the front desk here, Sir, Kiev is on the line."

What now?

"Who is it?"

"The Secretary of State for Home Affairs wants a word with
you, Your Excellency."

Trotskaya's cousin, now elevated to the inner ruling cabinet
of his country after the long night's re-shuffle hinted at by her
in Nice, was the new Secretary of State for Home Affairs. He'd
been instrumental in the promotional transfers to the Embassy
in New Delhi of the First Secretary and His Excellency.

"Good afternoon. Minister." It would be just after breakfast
in Kiev.

"Good morning, Your Excellency." In fact, night was falling
in New Delhi. This rigmarole meant recording devices could
stay off, as this was a personal call.

"You got Vera Natalya kitted up and saw her off?"

"We did. Taking a Buddhist booklet of mine with her,
Taming the Tiger, that I had given her in Nice."

"Bit of a non-starter, as a project, I would say, for my cousin."

164

"So it would seem."

"Look, Your Excellency, I'm phoning because we thought we'd located her, we were sure in fact. After much wandering about, she finally settled down near Bangalore, in a place called Namdroling."

"How'd you find that out?"

"We tagged her back-pack."

"You didn't. You told me yourself that she wanted..."

"We told you that, yes. But don't forget she's family, your Excellency. I didn't want outsiders of any description to know of her whereabouts, as she insisted she was on a spiritual quest. She tried once to explain it to me. I didn't get the hang of it. I've always thought that reality is to be lived, not to be the object of thought and meditation."

> *That cousin must have got a belly-full*
> *about her attachments as well.*

"I got hints of all this myself during our brief acquaintance, Minister, and I agree. It's simply no good detaching from reality altogether, by sitting under a fig tree all day. Couldn't make head nor tail of that, like you. I'd bought this booklet, "Taming the Tiger" but it didn't help at all, so I gave it to her."

"Anyway," Home Affairs continued, "after a few weeks, she started moving around in a very erratic way and now the tag's gone dead. That can only mean someone's stolen her backpack and taken it out of the country, but she still has her wallet and credit card in a body bag. That's it. And it's not been used now for some time, so there's no knowing what's happened to her.

"Another reason I'm calling is that we've discovered that Branislav's remaining henchmen aren't bothered much about who murdered him or why. They're quite happy dividing his spoils up amongst themselves. And the French police, though her fingerprints are on the handle of the bayonet, couldn't care less about that either: glad to have another trans-national criminal out of the way."

"So Vera Natalya is no longer in any danger from them and

could safely come home to a very generous State Pension, richly deserved, should she so wish. And I wish she would. If she ever turns up, would you put it to her?"

"Certainly, Minister. But there's no sign of her at all at this end. But we do have something of interest to report. We've her boyfriend in the Embassy here, under our Political Asylum, at this very moment."

"Since when? She never once mentioned a boyfriend to me. How does he fit into the picture?"

This was explained, leaving out any reference to a new pulp novella in His Excellency's pipeline. It's authors having agreed, over more cognac, to keep all the lust, intrigue, bare flesh and love-child interest in (including the rivettingly successful DNA denouement), but to set the whole story, under assumed names, in Glenrothes amongst the humpy hills of Fife and call it the *Thirty-nine Stupes*.

And as His Excellency was nearing the end of his tale, which had taken some time in the telling, the clerk on duty in the foyer of the Embassy picked up the red phone. Finding it still engaged with the Principal Author's narrative, he sent a messenger up to the Ambassadorial office. Who said that an attractive woman calling herself Vera Natalya Trotskaya, claiming to be a Ukranian national, but with neither passport nor appointment, had just presented herself at the front desk to ask if His Excellency could spare a moment.

On they Rowed

ACCORDING TO KLOSEN QUANTAS

A LA RECHERCHE DU NYL YDASSAC

Re-introducing the "peat generation", a picayune & picaresque grouping of mix'n'match anti-intellectuals & philo-sofas with a shared interest in partially decayed vegetation and striving towards a mystic oneness with the great cosmic Bud, often using unorthodox methodology. This includes the widespread adoption of false names to give their work(s) a veneer of exogenous authenticity. For example, Klosen Quantas, (see above) in fact has a passport in the name of Bjorn Egin, and holds a proper day job as caretaker of the chicken runs at the Norwegian mission. The other leading figures in the movement, (if you can call it that, many of them sit about in bars playing music all day) are Kcaj Macauorek, the child bride Binty, and her long lost step-father, the notoriously transitional bearded poet Nella Grebsnig. With their legalization as gurus and pioneers of coffee grounds, a new street memoir seems timely.

THE FIRST TIME I ran into Nella Grebsnig I was in a stolen jalopy and it was lucky one of the wheels came off or I'd have broken his leg. Binty, in the back seat, was feeding her step sister's baby and counting a wad of ten pound notes she'd found in the glove compartment. The tight jeans round Nella's arse caught her eye immediately.

"Where'd you get the gun?" she said through mauve shades.

"The last train to San Fernando," mouthed the beard.

"Cute. But there's no station stop at San Fernando. And never was. What's the game, beardo? It's the name of a song isn't it? You some kind of lay-down-your-head Tom Dooley?"

"When the night train stops near San Fernando is where I make the jump. It's a hobo junction. A guy there gave me the gun for a mass of mary jane I had on me. Dig?"

"That's my kind of music, beardo. Catholic, sacred and profane. Get on in. We'll take you there."

I could see right off that it was match on for Binty and Nella by the way they spoke to each other in quotes from corny old folk songs of a by-gone era. A trick we'd gotten off a muscular but shy photographer way up in Canada, name of Jock Carroll.

"But the car's just lost a fucking wheel," said Nella, "So, what are you two on, stems and seeds? I was told that if I went down to the woods to-day, I'd be sure of a big surprise."

"There aren't any woods round here. This is mainland Plobster. It's a peatbog leading to a fracking-oil refinery."

"That's not what the captain said on the ferry coming over."

"That'll have been Kcaj, he's such a jerk," said Binty, while knocking off the last of the baby's Complan.

"Kcaj. Now that's a peculiar name to have."

"Kcaj Macauorek." I put in, "He poses as a shamanic Scots/Eskimo and makes up scenery and weather as he goes along for a living, loudly declaiming it to anyone who'll listen. If the weather and scenery turn out different to what he says, then he writes it all down anyway and sells it off, along with a whole heap of rude stories, at agricultural shows."

"Never."

"He does. He says some people find reading scenery and rude stories a lot better than hearing about it."

"He sure did convince me about those woods, I'll tell you. And in them he said was a shrine dedicated to a muse Goddess of Peotry. What was her name now...that I should visit...?"

"Nyl Ydassac?"

"That was it. The very one. Exactly. It was because of his recommendation that I was swinging low, lost in a day-dream, in the middle of the road, not thinking there'd be anyone riding around in an automobile, when suddenly..."

"Let's all head over the hill to Scurf Bay," I suggested on the spur of a moment to put an end to all this lyrical tripe, "grab a boat, row over to the 'Spit and Sawdust' bar on the Hoy of Noy and get boozed up."

"We can all stay in my step sister's yurt," Binty purred, while shoving the wad of tenners down her bra. "Kcaj's on in the bar tonight as it happens, singing the *Ballad of Nyl Ydassac* that he wrote about her. That'll be right up the street where you live, beardo."

"All one hundred verses," I pipped in, "unaccompanied."

"And more." Binty added, "there's no stopping Kcaj when he's on a roll about his beloved Nyl. Nylorac, that's the first name in full. You'll hear it mentioned. A good deal."

"Get me to the yurt on time then."

"By the way," Nella said as Binty took her shades off, "haven't we met somewhere else before...some place...somewhere?"

A few minutes pulling hard on the oars over to the Hoy of Noy thankfully put a full stop on any more of this garbage, at least for the time being. The slightest sniff of Johnny Cash and it would been over the side for both of them.

OH WHAT A NIGHT IT WAS, IT REALLY WAS, SUCH A NIGHT

INDEED, LATER that night, through the thick smoke and dungarees in the back room of the Spit and Sawdust, you could just make out the figures of the peat poets assembled there; the unravelled sleeves of their otherwise sturdy pullovers soaking up the beer spilled evenly on table and floor.

Angus McCockoffit, (whistle) Spotlis Leclean, (pipes and knee organ) Cannagh McTurtle, (tambourine and spoons) and Urs Shall-Notwndt (fiddle) as well as many others were present. Binty's toasted bannocks, made from herring veins and caramelised tootsies (home grown) were being chucked around with abandon; along with ham-fisted economics, venison cheapflights and alternative modes of liquid gas extraction. The joint was jumping.

"It was a night, ooo what a night it was, it really was, suchch a night." Binty coughed as she spluttered.

"19th nervous breakdown. Man, here it coooomes," Nella said, througing up in passable barber-shop harmony. This man/woman had obviously been around. More miles under the legs than you could shake a stick at.

Then, thank God, it was Kcaj's turn to sing and there was such a stampede for the outside shit-house that it drowned out any more of their febrile horseplay.

PUT YOUR HANDS TOGETHER THEN FOR A FRIEND OF US ALL KCAJ MACAUOREK AND THE BALLAD OF NYL YDASSAC

"She came from a high end fam-il-y who'd made it in rough trade. No cat meat in the gravy, no pith in the lemonade. But she lost her heart to a gambling man, who played with loaded dice. His first name was Charisma, his last was illegal highs.

Nyl Ydassac !! Nyl Ydassac !! Ach , whit a sonsie lassie.

Wi' a rum and a strum and a Highland Quorum,

clingin' tae yer chassis."

"This is sooo cool," said Binty.

Now Binty at that time was by no means what later came to be known as a "thinking man's crumpet". But she looked a fair treat feeding her step sister there in the murk while at the same time counting the cash she'd just nicked off a local anaesthetist asleep on the bench beside her.

After verse 10, came a break for more hooch 'n spice. Always quick out the box after a few gins, I put my pea in the pot.

"I wonder if Mr Tambourine Man would play a song for me?" Silence.

"In the jingle jangle morning...No? River High, Mountain Deep, then. Hic."

Silence.

Was it the other way round, I thought? River deep...? Christ, what's Binty put in these bannocks? Luckily, Nella took my toxic slather at face value and stepped right in, which was cool.

"Do you know the way to San Jose?" he queried with one eye in the general direction of Binty. Who was sulking so bad it left me still in contention.

"Yes, it's down in Savannah, eatin' cream and bananas, and the heat just makes me faint."

More silence. From both of them. Clearly not cool to do two lines of the same song in any one turn. Bugger. I lurched outside into the yard just in time to pee into a ditch and stare up in semi-dormant wonderment at the moon above which might've been a has-been can in the trees.

Soon after, Kcaj called it a day just short of his century and joined me outside with Binty and Nella clinging onto each other like ivy on a brick wall. "*C'est la vie*, said the old folks, it goes to show you never can tell," I chirruped to myself, attempting Chuck Berry's trademark ostrich walk in virtual reality.

When I found out about it later, it was me that had to tell Binty that Nella was in fact her long lost transitional step-father, which really put the cat amongst the hot tin roofs.

"Who made all those nail holes in the sky, letting in the light," asked a certain captain in the Peatish navy. This was hovering on the edge of prosody, where no birds sing. Some dude once said, probably with a tourniquet wrapped round his arm poor bastard, that the holes up there were to limit the amount of darkness that gets out; to keep more of it in.

I said, I reckoned ole' rat-face Dylan got it right when he called the night sky a "Highway of Diamonds with Nobody On It". Various dishevelled and sundry peat folk gathered round the shit-house muttered their agreement hoarsely as we threaded our way through the puke back to the bar.

What a night that was, it really was; such a night. Outside the Spit and Sawdust with Binty, Nella, Kcaj and his fabled muse Nyl Ydassac watching over him from her tin can in heaven with her white hair shining and her non-judgmental smile (verses 103-107, approximately, on most nights, in the summer months, depending).

GLOSSARY of every day terms. Soddenish Islands.

Boak	Belch, retch
Bourne	Burden
Broch	Large round tower w/hollow walls for hacking coughs
Chap	An upper class English male. A modest cut of beef, pork or lamb
Choulched	A pin-stripe jaw strap or bridle. Ass's choker
Chowk	(ditto)
Fiscal	Prosecution lawyer in the lowers courts
Froch	Short fisherman's oiled jersey
Hoch	Upper part of hind leg. Plentiful sputum
Hochcgh	(ditto)
Homo hubris	Tight fisted, bottle browed indiginous hominid Cleaned out by Homo slopiens
Hotching	Itching, scratching
Hugger-mugger	Furtive, untidy, prone to cabal
Hurdies	Buttocks, hips, haunches
Kelty	A salmon or sea trout heading seawards An alcoholic drink forced on an abstainer
Lallans	A "lowland" language. As opposed to a "highland" language such as Gaelic
Merk	A discontinued coinage. Thick Fog
Midden	Compost heap. A gluttonous animal or vegetable.
Ming	Stinking
Pouk	Unfledged feathers of a miserable fowl. To clutch or pick at.
Rhoddie	Obscure. Children were said to be spoiled if it was spared. Rubber ones more flexible.
Scraggs	Stunted, shrivelled. Often covered with under growth
Scroggs	(ditto)
Screes	A mass of loose stones. Bars for riddling coal at the pit-head and relaxation after

Semmit	Long fisherman's undershirt. Worn by land lubbers too.
*Shreive**	Sherriff. Judge in the lower courts
Snot	Membranous mucus. The burned wick of a candle made from focus oil
Sonsie	(Of females) Honest, jolly, buxom Overlapped corner of a grocer's package
Spout	Water issuing from a cliff top cleft
Welsh rabbit	Unattributable
Yet	A natural pass between hills. (Nothing to do with football or consenting foreplay)

GAZETTEER of natural features (& places of interest SODDENISH ISLANDS

Ach	Often misty
Achnoe	Heavy mist frequently
Bachtofrontsay	Bespoke tailoring
Bog O' Bru	Stalled chambers. Road to the Ales
Bog O' Bigbag	Chambered stalls
Cottage Rhubha Duibhdhub	Sauna lease soon available
Eillan Taheelanto	Spring Festival of Raucus dancing
Filla	Famous rounded point
Flugga	Home for lost ingrates
Foulis Blister	Extinct cardboard hostages
Grunting Voe	Choking seals
Half Yell	Choking lobsters
Hisbigsister	Sibling freezer facility
Isthisbigster	Sports goods. Prophylactics
Knap of Horsenannies	Outspoken school of poetics
Kippa Cnocen	Freemasons only. Tiers of historic drainage
Mousevista	Cheese with a view.
Neck of Stocinis	Calf-length boutique
of Scrootinis	Covert CCTV tax exemption centre

Pewllagh Plugga	Peat poet ceilidhs
Rubha Moethball	Puffins. Northernmost knitting known-
Scabs of Mouster	Muffins. Entire cattle
Scyrf O' Skerries	Puffed wiffins. (Abandoned hair pieces)
Udairsay	Squabbling plutocrats
Voe of Hoota	Padded cells for Celtic tonsure, sirens
of Habstinis	Centre for addictive behaviours

POPULAR UK BRAND NAMES
IF UNKNOWN, NOT EMBARGOED

Balkan Sobranie	. Strong cigarettes for the sophisitcate
Tunnocks	Family baker in Uddingston of caramel fame
Locozade	Energy and sports drink
Horlicks	Malted milk drink
Ephgrave	Sturdy pre-WWII bicycle
Goratox	Gore Tex in disguise
Brompton	Folding bicycle
Durex	Condoms, washable varieties discontinued
Complan	Powdered milk energy drinks

*Glossary note: "Smuir" is Scots for shite. Anything smelling of shit is said to be "mingin'". Shrieve is coloquial for a Sheriff who presides as Judge in the lower Scottish courts for minor criminality. The Fiscal is the law officer in the Sheriff court acting, on behalf of the Crown, for the prosecution.

ENCORE

BESIDE
the
SEASIDE

A SMELLODRAMA

BRIGHTLY LIT STAGE WITH MANY COLOURFULL TENTS, WINDBREAKS, ETC. SPACE DOWNSTAGE FOR TWO FOLDING DECK-CHAIRS TO BE BROUGHT ON BY THE ACTORES. SOUNDS OF SURF BREAKING IN THE DISTANCE AND OCCASIONAL SEAGULL SQUAWKS THROUGHOUT THE PLAY.

THE FARTS, VARYING IN PITCH AND LENGTH, PRE-RECORDED, SHOULD APPEAR TO BE COMING FROM SOMEWHERE BEHIND AN ONSTAGE TENT/ WINDBREAKS PLACED MIDWAY BETWEEN THE TWO ACTORS WHEN SEATED IN THEIR DECK-CHAIRS. IT'S JUST FEASIBLE THEN, TO START WITH, FOR EACH OF THEM TO ASSUME (AND REACT) AS IF THE OTHER IS DOING THEM.

DIFFERENT WAYS OF REACTION SUGGEST THEMSELVES. THE LIST IS NOT EXCLUSIVE. BOTH CHARACTERS CARRY ON WITHOUT INTERRUPTION, POLITELY PRETENDING, WITH COMIC "DISPLACEMENT" BUSINESS, THAT NOTHING HAS HAPPENED. THE FARTS CAN OCCUR IN NATURAL PAUSES, WITH OR WITHOUT REACTION, OR CAUSE A PAUSE IN THE DIALOGUE, AS EACH MOMENTARILY REGISTERS THE OCCURRENCE OF AN UNEXPECTED AND POTENTIALLY EMBARRASSING SITUATION THAT HAS PROBABLY BEEN CAUSED BY THE OTHER PERSON.

Enter, from opposite directions, two senior citizens, a "white" male (A) and "non-white" female (B). Each carries a folded deck chair, and a light canvas bag with the day's kit. Clothing is beach kitsch, especially the hat and sunglasses. which can be adjusted and taken on and off throughout.

A   Cleo! Head nurse, Ear Nose and Throat.
B   Dr McCaliper, I presume, if I'm not mistaken.
A   It's been a few years. **Fart**
B   Too right. What a surprise.
A   Were you thinking of roosting here today yourself?
B   I was, in fact. How unbelievable. This'll be nice.

They unfold their deckchairs and sir down

A   How you keeping? **Fart**
B   Well. Thank you.

A   And your brother, the Lord Chief Justice?

B   Died on the table. **Fart**

A   Oh. And then there was that Kathy **Fart** whats-her-name. Did the bloods on the your ward....

He discretely fans himself with his hat.

B   Slipped and broke her neck unfortunately. Nursing in the Olympic village.

A   No. The last place you'd expect...

B   You wouldn't, no.

A   Very often the case. In our **Fart** line of business.

He sneezes several times.

B   True. And your mother? I well remember that evening.

A   One of many

B   It certainly was **Fart**

A   Eventually went in for a different business altogether.

B   Digestive biscuits wasn't it?

She rummages around in her beach bag.

      Here, have one.

A   Thank you. Something very like it yes. On a large scale. Huge plant. **Fart**

B   So I heard.

She get out of her chair.

      Now look here. This just can't go on.

A   What?

B   This...these...Are you sure you're all right?

A   These what? Whatever do you mean? **Fart**

B   That's what I mean. I thought it might be you. Now don't get me wrong, Dr McCaliper

A   Me?

B   I really don't mind at all...except that....

Dr Caliper gets out of his chair.

A   Are you accusing me....

B   It's better not to hold onto it But on the other hand....

A   It can't possibly have been me.

A pause, as they both face each other in silence. **Fart**
Neither moves then both burst out laughing.

A   It's someone else, isn't it.

He wanders over to the other side of the stage and points directly at the audience.

            I think it's coming from over there.

B   No. They're coming from over here. **Fart** That proves it.

A   Well it can't be me then because I'm standing over here.
            It's obviously been you all along. I was beginning
            to think so. And you have the nerve to...

Gigantic Fart *followed, from the same location as the farts, by the sound of something falling heavily to the ground with a hard crack.*

B   Whatever was that?

A   Sounded to me very like someone crapping themselves
            and collapsing.

B   Dead?

A   Sounded very like it. I once worked in a prison.

B   It could have been a sack of potatoes falling though.
            Best not to interfere. Whatever it is of course
            might still be alive. Getting the barbie ready.

As they arrange themselves back in their chairs, they whisper furtively, as if the farter might be listening to them. Cleo gets a small purse out of her bag with a folding mirror and some lipstick in it.

A   And if so and he's only just dropped the spuds for the
barbie as you say, then he's bound to do another...you know...
            wollopper sooner or later.

B   Then we'll know. Yes. We could of course ask him or her.

A   Perhaps we could simply...go round and see...for our
            selves what's... going on.

B   I don't want to see it. With or without jacketed potatos.
            Lets wait here, as you say, for a bit. Then decide
            what's best to do.

She finishes her make-up and replaces everything in the purse
which she holds in her lap, She then leans back and dies peace-
fully. One lifeless arm drops down and swings momentarily.
The other remains in her lap holding the purse.

A   It was you that said that I think. You know I'm beginning
          to wonder......

He gets up feverishly, muttering to himself, and offering Cleo
assistance, oblivious that she's dead.

          ...if we shouldn't quietly remove ourselves from
          round here before the balloon goes up if you see
          what I mean...about what's going on...Here, let
          me help you with your things. Whatever has
          happened over there...Are these yours? There's
          going to be a major hoo-hah (*sneezes*) the police,
          the whole lot. And, as well as that, after that last
          one, there'll be an awful mass of *hic* muck lying
          around out here, (*burps*) seeping out everywhere,
          carrying all manner of god knows what. Here's
          your bag.

He removes the make-up purse from her hand and puts it in her
bag. That arm flops lifelessy down like the other.

A   I'll put that in here. Christ it's getting hot. Let me give
          you a hand with your deck chair. No? Look,
          there's no point in staying here Cleo,whatever the
          circ *burp* um *hic* umstances. Are you listening?
          Look I think I'll just take a short waaaalk, get the
          shirt off and cool down with a nice swim no
          problem. Slight headache. Then come back and
          catch you later no problem.

Getting out of breath, he hurries offsatge with his chair in the
opposite direction from which he came on.
From this offstage location there is the sound of a loud fart,
a strangled gasp and something falling heavily to the ground
as before.

A single loud seagull squawk.

LIGHTS OUT SUDDENLY.

In the blackout Cleo leaves the stage, also in the opposite direction from which she came on, carrying her chair and bag with her.

As soon as she's offstage, the lights (and seaside sounds) come abruptly back on again.

After a short pause, both actores re-enter from where they left the stage and the whole play is repeated, word for word WITH THE ACTORES SWOPPING ROUND ROLES. THE FEMALE PLAYS "A" (DR McCALIPER) AND THE MALE "B" (CLEO) THE HEAD NURSE. He can be re-named Fred.

"Business" can be more or less replicated according to taste. At the end, the male actor can substitute sun-tan cream for lipstick and die with the tube in his hand.